OBSIDIAN OF RUBY

Grey Liliy

BROKEN POCKET

ISBN-13: 978-1943161034
ISBN-10: 1943161038

Cover Illustration by Malwina "Rothinsel" Pokusinska

Cover Design by Grey Liliy

Table of Contents

Prologue

THE AIR TASTED like ash in her mouth, the dry bitterness clinging to her tongue like an unwanted kiss.

Lady pushed the scalding hot wood of the broken door off her back. She coughed through the smoke in her lungs, forcing it out with hacking breaths that made her ribs shake. The bulk of the obstruction clattered to her side, sparks shooting up from the smoldering wood as it snapped in half. The planks sizzled, smoke rising as bits of orange and yellow light escaped the wooden cracks threatening to ignite. Lady picked herself up before it could catch fire, and climbed out of the wreckage of her once home. Free from the collapsed walls and roof, she looked up.

The air was red, a sky of burning orange and brilliant ruby.

It would have been glorious, if not for the screams and burnt flesh covering the ground below it. Lady's eyes watered as she swallowed down her fear and moved forward. The world was already on fire, how much worse could it be? Lady's ears rang from all the noise as she shoved through the warm and panicked bodies, pushing past her friends and neighbors, looking for any sign of her father in the chaos. Lady covered her mouth, squinting through the smoke that settled around her. Trying to see past the waistlines and belts that kept getting in her way was near impossible, and for the first time Lady cursed her height.

When she became an adult, surely she wouldn't still be this short!

Lady shook her head to clear the useless thoughts as she passed the burning buildings and kept searching. Her father had to be here somewhere. He was always on his way home around this time, and he'd be halfway to their house on the dot if he was on time. If he was late, it was because he had stopped by the baker to pick up sweet buns. Her father had to still be on his way; there was no chance he'd have stopped for sweets! Lady couldn't have missed him!

A shriek of broken glass filled the air, a hideous screech like the sound of a thousand porcelain plates crashing to the ground and shattering all at once. Lady sucked in a breath, not ready for another round of fire so soon after the last blast. She ducked close to the ground, covering her head on instinct. She clamped her eyes shut, and dug her fingers hard into her hair as she waited.

Lady whined when another screech of glass sounded overhead.

A burst of fire surged at her side, the force of it throwing her on her back. Lady screamed as it past her, a boiling and bubbling heat that was far too close. She rolled over clutching her face and hissing hard from the lick of flame that had eaten away at her side. The slightest touch of that fire was enough to steal half of her face and arm, the skin cooked like roast meat.

Lady surged to her feet, only to trip back down to her knees. She breathed hard in and out as best as she could in almost a mantra of air, trying to fight through the pain with gasping breaths as her skin continued to burn. This would be alright. She'd be okay. Father was always saying things like that. Like when she broke her arm climbing trees. It was just a break. Just pain. It would heal. Lady sniffled and felt her heart beating faster as her fingers found the tender, exposed skin. She pressed into the numb flesh, and hitched her breath. Lady shook her head, tugging on the burnt flesh from the healthy remaining. She stood up, eyes open. It was just a burn. Surely it was just a—

A deafening roar called out over the land, a sound that rang out with the power of a deity's shout.

Lady dropped her hands, bits of blood bubbling in her burnt flesh as she looked toward the sky. Giant black wings opened wide and covered the ground around her in shadow. The obsidian scales scratched against each other, filling the air with that cursed sound of broken glass that made her ears want to bleed. This was no silent killer, and for once, Lady wished that he was. His scales were cracked and covered in spider-web fractures, shining and sparkling in the fire light with a beauty that beast had no right to. She turned her head as the monster landed on the town's church tower: Brilliant, large and looming. It sat still as a statue, bringing a halt to the screeching scales. Lady stood, her hands gripping tightly in the apron at her waist. Her tiny form a spec in the sea of adults and people frozen in place as it watched them all.

For a few fleeting moments, all was silent as they stared at their tormenter:

A Great Dragon.

Lady breathed in awe of his size and power, but she made the mistake of looking down. The smoky air filled her lungs with her gasp. Lady covered her mouth with both hands in an instant as her shoulders shook and her eyes watered.

There just beneath the Dragon, near the opening to the church was a familiar white shirt on the back of a dead man with dark hair. A shirt with delicate red roses embroidered into the collar and side of his sleeves. Even from a distance, the pattern was unmistakable. Lady swallowed her choked sob, and dropped her head down to stare at her feet in the scorched dirt.

Her father wasn't coming home.

The monster flapped his wings hard, and shook himself off like a lazy cat. The sound drew Lady's attention as a shower of broken glass scales fell from his body. They shredded anything that they touched, sharp as knives. Even Lady's father. Her brown eyes widened as new cuts covered her father's corpse, dying his favorite shirt in red blood.

Teeth clenched, Lady screamed back at him as he dived from the church for another round of destruction:

"I'm going to kill you!"

Chapter 1

ONCE UPON A time, there was a brilliant valley of roses and they were very special.

Instead of soft petals and sweet scents, they were made of brilliant ruby gemstones. Their emerald stems, covered in sharp protruding thorns, shot up from the earth in batches of the hundreds. They were lovely things, every stem held a single precious flower with delicate petals cut from thin slices of the red gem. The entire floor of the valley was covered in them, more than any human could ever count.

These flowers were the most beautiful the world had ever seen, and would most certainly have been coveted by all if anyone had known they were there.

"Dragons are nothing more than pure evil! Selfish, greedy monsters with wings that have no heart, no mercy and, and worse! Their icy hearts are so frozen that they're too cold for even the winter!" Lady shouted. She slammed her beer mug on the bar counter, sloshing the liquid over the edge and onto the dingy wooden surface. Lady hiccuped lightly, and drank another deep gulp from her cup. She hummed with a smile as she wagged a finger back and forth in the air. "Which is impressive for something that's innards are on fire, don't you think?"

Her companion that occupied the bar seat to her left, a total stranger in decorated silver armor, paused mid sip of his decidedly fancier drink in a short glass. He lifted a delicately formed eyebrow up into his neat black hairline as he pondered her statement. He snorted into his glass and grinned widely, showing off his pearly white teeth. "I would not disagree with you. They are rather wretched, aren't they?"

"The absolute worst," Lady said, sipping the last of her drink. She held her chin up, and smacked the counter with her palm for a refill for her ale. The bartender rolled his eyes, but took her glass to fill it to the brim anyway. Lady tapped her index finger on the bar next to his elbow as matter-of-fact as she could. "Which is why I kill them."

"Seems as good a reason as any," he replied, tapping his own fingers on the bar in a relaxed, bored rhythm.

"Well you know what I do for a living," Lady said. The man next to her had a strong roman profile, and a hint of muscle in that lean form. He was good looking enough, sure, but it wouldn't hurt to learn a little bit more about him, would it? Lady rubbed her palm on the side of her armor, scratching her finger into the dip of a scratch marring the metal surface. "You've only been listening to me ramble for the past hour. So how about you, Mr. Shining Armor? What do you do?"

"I'm nothing but a spoiled brat, I'm afraid," he said. He tapped the edge of the delicate engravings of his armor. The thin lines carved out a beautiful field of roses and fierce wolves over the surface. It was rather romantic for someone whose demeanor seemed to hint at someone rather icy. He rubbed off a smudge of dirt from his shoulder. "The perfectly polished armor didn't give you a hint? I thought dragon slayers were observant."

"Oh, I noticed," Lady said, touching her finger to a perfectly formed rose on his chest. The pattern was familiar, and Lady shoved down the memory as hard as she could. It wasn't exactly the same. Just a rose. Lady pressed her lips together, and rested her arms on the counter. "I'm just wondering what line of work would have someone as tidy as you running around in a full suit of armor."

"I like how it looks," he said, with a deadpan seriousness that made her want to giggle. The hint of humor behind it was intriguing, and a brownie point if Lady had ever given one. She leaned harder on the counter, turning to face the man more. He definitely could be fun for at least a night. Lady had time for that much, didn't she? The man turned back to his glass, and took a heavy gulp of the liquid showing off the skin of his neck peaking out of the top of his shirt under the armor. He tapped the side of his chest plate and asked, "Do I need a better reason?"

"I suppose I can deal with that for now," Lady said, clicking her tongue. She rested her chin in her hand, smiling quietly to herself. Lady most certainly had time for a bit of company. For tonight, anyway. She rubbed a small circle into a section of smooth flesh on her scarred cheek. "If I can't get a job out of you, how about a name?"

The stranger stared at the far wall, almost as if he hadn't heard Lady's question. He turned his glass lightly on the counter, attempting to look bored. Though Lady could see it in his eyes that he was still paying attention. *Good.* He took a slow sip of his drink, and smiled as he finally answered, "Amadeus."

Lady repeated the name silently, sounding it out with her lips. She tilted her head to the side, spilling her braid over her shoulder. "That's an old name."

"A favorite of nobility," Amadeus said, "to name things after ones long gone and traditional."

"I suppose that's true," she said. Lady sat up to see his face better. If he really was of that class, he'd have plenty of practice covering up his emotions. But Lady could tell that a few drinks had created cracks in that alternative armor of his. Lady wanted to see it break down even more, and asked, "Which nobility? I'm going to take it that 'Amadeus' is attached to a family name?"

He held a finger up to the tips of his lips, and shook his head with a dazzling smile that nearly blinded Lady. "Ah, now. How about a trade? You tell me your name first, and I might let you in on the spoiled brat's parentage."

"Lady," she replied, taking a gulp of her drink and wiping off the mustache of foam with the back of her hand. *Shit, he was cute.* Maybe she ought to cancel that one night plan. If he kept smiling like that, Lady might want to keep him—and that was something she really didn't have time for. He kept watching her, and she bit the edge of her lip. Though, maybe he had earned her name. "Lady of the Northern Falls, Fifth Family."

"Just 'Lady'?" He asked, using the same questioning tone as any other to hear her name. "Your name is as odd as mine is old if that's the case."

"But my name all the same," she said. Lady lightly shoved him in the shoulder, distracting him from the question and the oddity of her simple name. "Your House, I believe is what I'm owed for that information?"

"Of course," he tipped his head down in a delicate nod. He pressed a hand over his chest, and bowed further with a court-like grace. "Amadeus of the Ruby Mines, First Family, is pleased to make your acquaintance, Fair Lady of the Northern Falls."

"Ruby Mines?" Lady asked, her heart pounding against her ribs. She clenched the sides of her cup, her shoulders hunching inward. Lady swallowed, her teeth clenched. His handsome face melted away as a far more fearsome animal head entered her mind, flashing eyes of red. Lady bit her lip hard. "As in the Ruby Mines just north of the Emerald Plains?"

"The same," Amadeus said with a knowing smile, though she noted the hint of confusion in his eyes. He *was* good at hiding those things. Lady watched him close as he leaned back and held his hand up. "I'm not surprised you've heard of it. That entire area is rather famous for its most prestigious resident in our mountains. The—"

"Obsidian of Ruby," Lady said, finishing his sentence for him. She sat up straight, relaxing her shoulders as the memories came rushing to the forefront of her mind. Lady could never forget that dragon, or that night. Lady's knuckles turned white under her gloves, the armored metal rubbing lightly as it followed her fingers into a fist. "A Great Dragon with scales made of obsidian and eyes that shine like rubies. Famous for fires that burn as hot as a volcano's lava, and scales that shriek like broken glass when it moves. A dragon that has claimed the lives of over four thousand people across the Continent, double the kills of any other Great Dragon in this land."

"You've heard of him," Amadeus said, sipping his drink. He watched her from the corner of his eye, blocking out everything in the room. "While that doesn't fully surprise me, he is rather famous, you seem to be rather intimately acquainted with him considering the way your hands are trembling."

Lady let go of her glass, and held her hands together tightly.

"That monster murdered my father and destroyed my village when I was a little girl," Lady said.

She breathed in slowly and concentrated hard. It was just pain. It would pass. Just like her father always said that it would. Lady tossed her braid over her shoulder, smacking him lightly in the cheek with the edge of her hair band. Amadeus turned his head to face her, and Lady clicked her tongue. She knocked over her empty cup with a flick of her fingers, and pushed her long bangs back behind her ear.

The scar that covered the left half of her face, extending down her neck and onto her shoulder beneath the armor, didn't gather so much as a gasp or a blink for her drinking companion. That earned him a real smile on her face. "And I vowed to kill him."

Amadeus stared at her for a moment before he burst into laughter. Ruining her serious moment and drawing attention from the other patrons of the bar, Amadeus continued chortling hard enough that he had to cover his mouth with his hand to stifle it. Lady's heart skipped a beat at the wonderful sound that was his voice in joy.

Even if she could feel an equal amount of anger bubbling up for being laughed at.

Amadeus threw a few coins onto the table paying for his drink and stood up, still chuckling. He wiped a tear from the side of his eye and shook his head. He tapped his knuckles on the counter next to her elbow and whispered near the side of her ear, "I wish you luck with that, Lady. I really do."

"You didn't have to be rude about it!" Lady shouted at him as he walked away from the bar top.

Amadeus disappeared up the stairs toward the inn's rooms on the second floor, and Lady turned back to the bar. She slammed her hand on the counter. "Another drink!"

"Sunlight is the enemy," Lady hissed, shoving the limp, flat pillow over the top of her head.

The paper-thin beige curtains did nothing to block out the morning light, and said shining rays were more than happy to flood her bed and room with their obnoxious brightness. They beat down on her back for another ten minutes before Lady sat up in bed, unable to stand the hot sun on her nightgown any longer. She scratched the side of her head, and yawned into her hand. A tangle-battle with the sheets ended with Lady on her feet, her auburn hair in her face, and the sheets defeated on the floor.

She exhaled a deep sigh, staring intently at the empty space on the other half of the bed. She shoved her loose hair back over her head and dragged her fingers through the tangles. Even with that odd moment when he'd laughed at her, Lady had been hoping for a little longer company with her new acquaintance from last night. But Mr. Shining Armor clearly had better things to go do after her declaration of dragon murder than coming back upstairs with Lady to her room.

They were always doing that.

Lady snorted, and threw the sheets back on the bed. One day she'd meet a man who didn't run away when she told them her life goals!

Not that it made her feel any less bitter. Lady splashed her face with the lukewarm water in her wash bowl, and rubbed away the sweat from her sleep. No need to linger on it when the sun was up and her stomach was growling. It was another day, which meant another warm inn breakfast that would soon find its way to her belly. Who needed a man in your bed when there was food downstairs waiting?

The wonderful smell of sugared porridge drifting up through the floorboards got her back into armor and heading downstairs with a skip in her step. Her rucksack of belongings bounced on her back as she walked into the main hall without a hint of sleep lingering. This was just what she needed to clear her head of any distractions.

Now if only they'd stop showing up and getting in her way.

Lady bit the side of her lip when she saw a certain bar companion of hers from last night sitting off to the side of one of the long tables. With a full plate of sausage and eggs, no less.

The handsome bastard saw her, and had the nerve to smile her way.

Not one to pass up on second chances, the day was still early after all, Lady felt no shame helping herself to a seat across from him. In the full light of the day, her scratched and darkened armor looked every bit as old and worn as it was when compared to his almost glittering metal suit. She cleared her throat, and waved behind her to the rest of the room. "What sort of noble not only drinks with us low peons, but also helps himself to our breakfast?"

"A very bored one," Amadeus answered, cutting into his sausage. He took a bite with those lovely white teeth of his, and Lady was treated to a glimpse of green eyes when he looked up. "Wonderful to see you sober, my dear."

"It's been known to happen," Lady said, calling over her shoulder for porridge and a glass of juice. She put an elbow on the table, and sat her chin in her hand, her curled fingers sitting on the edge of her bottom lip. "Staying in town long?"

"Not very," Amadeus said. He brushed his hair back, and went back to cutting up his sausage into neat slices. The juice from each cut dripped onto his plate, showing off the innards of the delicious meat. Amadeus ate the piece from the end with a gentle shrug of his shoulders. "I never stay in one place for too long. Not when traveling, anyway."

"Because home is always home?" Lady asked, helping herself to a slice of his sausage while she waited. He frowned at her, but said nothing at her thievery. It tasted every bit as good as it looked. Lady licked her lip and took another piece. The huff that followed when the food disappeared behind her lips was worth it. "I can see that."

"Don't you have someplace to be?" Amadeus asked. A sliver of black hair escaped the slicked back style and fell between his eyes as he rested his chin on his hand. He twirled a finger around next to his cheek. "Dragons to kill, other fine inn patrons to bother?"

"I'm not sure," Lady said playfully, yet inwardly cursing herself. What was she doing? Lady needed to get on the road, not spend all her time trying to flirt with someone who wasn't interested. She kept going, despite her inner struggles. Green eyes were such a weakness for her! Lady clicked her tongue, "I'll have to pencil them in. Interesting men in armor take precedence, you know."

"Just the ones in armor, or just the rich men in armor?" He chuckled, warm and bright enough to rattle the metal plates he wore. Amadeus stuck a sausage with his fork and handed it across the table. "Or maybe just men with food?"

"Could be any combination of the three—"

"Dragon!" A man shouted, bursting into the inn. He stumbled over a stool at the front near the bar, and clutched to it like a crutch to keep from toppling over. His clothes were ruffled, and his breathing was jagged like he had run a few miles at least. The man looked up, and pointed behind him. "Flying this way!"

"Suppose that's a call for you," Amadeus said, humming lightly as he ate another bite of his sausage. He placed his silverware on his plate, and laced his fingers together on the table. "It'll be nice to see if your stories from last night are as true as you made them appear."

Lady pulled the sword off the back of her bag, and attached it tightly to her belt. *Perfect!* This was perfect. Nothing like killing a dragon to remind you there were better things in life than a pretty face. She held the handle tight as she looked over her shoulder. Though Lady wouldn't deny, impressing that pretty face as well sure wouldn't hurt! Lady winked. "Just you watch and see."

"Glad to," Amadeus said. The challenging smile that followed raised Lady's pulse, and she couldn't help but respond with one of her own.

Lady turned and jumped up and off the bench, her armor clanking loudly as the plates shifted. She rushed to the door, weaving in and out of the patrons as they abandoned their porridge and sausage, hand on her sword and head in the game. Until she got a good grip on the situation, she would have no idea if she was dealing with a quick kill, or if she'd have to start helping evacuate civilians before the throw down. Lady passed the messenger, and was out the door ready for anything.

The sun beat down on her head, the sky clear of clouds. Lady grabbed a tie from her side pack, and quickly pulled her hair up into a bun out of her face. People ran in her direction, frightened by something in the distance. It wasn't quite an unruly mob yet, but add a few more people and it would get there. She avoided the crowd, ducking off to the side walls of the buildings to get a better view. Lady scanned the horizon for the source of their fear, but she hadn't quite spotted it just—

"Northeast, just beyond the bell tower," Amadeus said, interrupting her thoughts and walking up to her side with her bag in his hand. He lifted a hand to shield his eyes from the daylight and whistled. "He looks angry."

Sure enough, in the direction that Amadeus had indicated was the beast's silhouette in the sun. Its wings flapped hard against the breeze, and it closed in on the town at a decent pace.

Lady dropped her shoulders, rolling her eyes to the side. She crossed her arms and walked at a leisurely pace toward the approaching beast. Lady snorted, "Just a wyvern, and not even a big one."

"It is annoying when people get them mixed up, isn't it?" Amadeus asked, following her about a step behind. Lady glanced at him from the corner of her eye. He was so calm, all considering. A wyvern was no concern for an experienced dragon slayer, but they were still dangerous to civilians. And here he was, calm as a cucumber. Amadeus hauled her bag up and threw it over his shoulder. "Though I suppose it's easy to miss from the distance."

"I'm impressed you recognized it," Lady said. She weaved her way around the people heading past her in the opposite direction in a panic. Lady kept her eyes on the approaching wyvern, making note of his increasing pace and the hints of fire coming from his mouth. The beastie was ready and on the attack, but it was hardly the only one. Lady drew her sword from its sheath when she arrived in the town clearing, the blade shining in the sun as she continued to walk. "Have more experience with dragons than you decided to share last night?"

"I own a library or two in my vast wealth, I have plenty of free time to read said books, and I live about two miles from one of the most ferocious dragons we've ever seen in this world," Amadeus said, licking the corner of his mouth. He shifted her bag, and shook his head with a laugh. "Take a wild guess at what qualifies as scary to me."

"You don't have to be so snippy about it," Lady said, knocking over a barrel with her foot. She rolled it about ten feet in front of her, and dropped her boot on the side to stop it from rolling. The wyvern came in fast, and would land any second. Lady turned to her almost unwanted companion, and raised an eyebrow. "Going to stick around for this? Or shouldn't you be taking cover, Mr. First Family?"

"For a wyvern of that size?" Amadeus asked, holding his free hand over his chest. "And with the company of a dragon slayer as decorated as you claim? What worry should I have?"

"At least step back," Lady said. *Cheeky brat*, she thought to herself, licking the side of her mouth. Lady turned a bit and shooed him away with her hand, flicking her fingers at him. "So you don't get in my way."

"Naturally."

Amadeus obediently walked backwards until he leaned against the wall of the nearest building. The town center, now home to a fountain, a dragon slayer, a barrel, and a spectator, was ready and waiting for its approaching pest. Lady reached into the pack that hung at her waist, and dug around through its contents. Lady had a surefire way to get the beastie's attention and make sure he dropped down in the empty square instead of the populated inns and homes.

"Hey!" Lady shouted at the top of her lungs. She thrust a handful of golden necklaces, each decorated with gems and other shiny things into the air. Lady shook it back and forth, making sure it caught both the sunlight and the light reflecting in the sparkling fountain water. "Come and get it!"

The sun glinting off the gold caught the wyvern's eye as it flew over the square, and it circled back around in a quick jerk. Its tin, green-colored scales were tinted in red at the edges and in splotches all over its back, giving it the appearance of a rusted child's toy, only a hundred times the size. Or larger. Lady guessed her quarry was about the size of a small elephant, either way. Close enough. She drew her sword with the other hand, and clutched the jewels tighter in her fist.

The wyvern dropped onto the center fountain, clutching to the statue of the town's mayor with the claws of its two wings. It opened its mouth, revealing rows of mismatched teeth and a forked tongue. Its twin tails whipped behind it back and forth on the street as its feet splashed in the water. The wyvern roared loudly, eyes locked on the golden necklaces in Lady's hands.

"You want them?" She asked, shaking her hand and jingling them together. The wyvern's eyes followed each movement, as greedy as any of its dragon cousins. Lady tossed the jewelry up and down in her hand. "Come and get them!"

The wyvern dove for her.

"Well that was anticlimactic," Amadeus said, stepping over the thickest part of the dead wyvern's second tail. The beast's first one hung across the the fountain where it had landed when Lady cut it off. Amadeus strolled alongside the spilled innards of the beast decorating the stone road, occasionally nudging them aside with the side of his boot. "That didn't even take you five minutes. Not even a fight worth retelling, really."

"It was just a wyvern," Lady said. She wiped the sizzling blood off her sword and whipped her towel hard in the air to get rid of the beaded droplets. They splashed onto the ground, and re-beaded near instantly. Lady slid her sword back into its sheath with a firm click. "Hardly worth the effort it took to kill it. I could have shooed it away, scaring it off, and the results would have been the same!"

"I wouldn't say that," Amadeus said. He knelt down and pulled out a small knife from a holster on his belt, the hilt inlaid with small gemstones. He pushed a bit of skin aside from Lady's final blow, a large slash in the side of the neck above the wyvern's protective scales, and shoved the knife inside. Bits of blood sizzled on his armor, but his thick gloves and metal protected his skin as he pulled the knife down. "Even the little ones like to collect."

Coins, gems and trinkets of all sizes spilled out onto the ground from the opening, covered in a thin layer of mucous. Amadeus shook the freed sack of flesh, knocking out the rest into the growing pile. When the last of it was out, he cleaned his knife on a handkerchief and replaced it on his belt. He tugged on the edge of the mucous and tossed the lump of it aside on the street. Mostly cleared of the gunk, Amadeus brushed aside the coins, and dug deep into the pile. Lady leaned over his shoulder just as he held up a rather large ruby in the air.

"Come on now," Lady said, "those aren't ours. We should return all of it to the town that thing just came from."

"Nonsense," Amadeus said. He held the gem up higher in the air, tilting his head just to the side. His eyes searched over every side of the ruby, concentrating on each surface. Amadeus pressed his lips together as a sly smile spread across his face. "Dragons and wyverns are hardly the only creatures in this world attracted to shining rocks and gold."

"That doesn't change my point," Lady said, shaking her head. She walked away from him, pulling her hair free from the bun. The braid fell over her shoulder, and she walked over to the fountain to wash off her face and armor.

"And my point," Amadeus said, tossing the gem up once before catching it. He joined her at the fountain and rinsed off his hand and the gem in the water. Amadeus' shoulder brushed hers as he leaned back. "Is that the people who owned these are most likely dead, and I'm rather fond of rubies."

"You don't know that for sure," Lady said. She pointed at him and then the stack of treasure. "That needs to be returned."

"You're free to do whatever you'd like with everything else, but this one I am keeping." Amadeus slipped the large gem into a pouch on the other side of his belt, and tipped his head toward Lady as he passed. "Wonderful meeting you, my dear. I do hope we meet again."

Lady bit the edge of her thumb through her gloves and watched the man walk off down the street.

The remainder of the wyvern's traveling hoard sat in the sun behind her.

Chapter 2

THE RUBY ROSES were secluded in a valley far, far away from all life aside from the small animals and insects that scurried about on the ground and flew overhead in the sky. Their beauty was beyond compare, and yet no one ever had the chance to appreciate them.

And they grew ever so lonely.

What good was being so desired, when there was no one to desire them? The roses wanted company to worship and adore them. Together as they grew in the sun, they decided that they would have it.

Nothing would stop them.

Lady yawned into her palm as she bounced up and down in the back of the rickety supply cart. The driver in the front seat hummed to himself with some dainty little tune as they traveled down the road, only stopping his rhythm to say a kind word or two to the horses drawing the cart. It wasn't bad enough that Lady ended up sleeping alone again after finding such a great catch, but she still wasn't able to find a decent form of transportation. Why must proper carriages be so expensive? Or handsome rich men so confusing?

She smacked both of her cheeks, and shoved Amadeus out of her mind. She didn't need that type of confusion in her life. He would have been a one night stand at best, and Lady shouldn't linger on him. She shifted her legs against the wooden boards of the floor. He wasn't worth it, and bumpy ride in a storage cart or not, there were better things out there for her.

Lady pushed up and leaned over the open edge, watching the fields of grapevines pass her by. This was real beauty: Handsome fields of fruit and gorgeous colors of purple and green. Lady inhaled deeply, loving the smell of the vineyards.

"Where you headed again?" The driver called over his shoulder. "Can't remember if I'm dropping you off up here at the South Vineyard when I drop off their supply order, or if you were riding with me to my next stop."

"South Vineyard is fine," Lady said. She pulled herself up and crawled toward the front of the cart, careful to keep her balance as the horses trotted along. Lady hauled herself up over the front edge and sat next to him in the passenger seat. She patted the comfy pillow cushion, and leaned back to cross her ankles on the foot rest. "I've already hitchhiked far enough on your generosity."

"Told you it was no trouble," he shrugged. "But if you insist."

Lady did.

As the cart crawled to a stop at the Vineyard's front gate, Lady hopped out of the seat and passed a few coins over into his hand. He thanked her with a tip of his hat and a smile, before continuing forward into the vineyard down the road. Lady hiked her travel pack higher over her shoulder and followed the rest of the road on foot. The main town for these fields shouldn't have been more than a mile or so down the road, if she remembered correctly.

Lady didn't visit the little Vineyard city often, but she should at least remember how far it was from the fields.

"I can not wait for a real bed again," Lady said to herself, yawning into her shoulder. Vineyard Acres had some of the best inns on the continent. Nothing like the flat, hard mattresses of the place she stayed last night. Lady rubbed her hands together and looked over the fields as she walked along the fence. The grapes were large and plump on the vine in hundreds of lush bunches, and she was tempted to reach across and steal a handful for a snack. She resisted, but barely. Lady scratched the back of her head, and pictured soft sheets and fluffy pillows instead. "A big soft one. Maybe I'll splurge and get a real suite with a full sized bed, instead of a standard single room with one of those wretched twins."

Lady blew her loose bangs out of her face and rolled her shoulders. Investing in a horse, or cart of her own was looking like the better and better option no matter what it cost her. Hitchhiking between towns was once no issue, but now it was becoming more of a bother than she cared to admit. At least then she'd have a better place to crash when on the road if she had a covered carriage or cart of some kind. It wouldn't be a bed, but a carriage cushion would be comfortable enough to sleep on. And there'd be a roof over her head! It would be far easier to travel on her own terms, even if it came with the downfall of stable fees and food for the horses.

But then again, having a horse meant she wouldn't have to walk the last few miles to town because she didn't want to be a burden to the nice man who gave her a lift.

Lady looked up at the blue sky overhead and breathed out softly. "At least the weather is nice."

"Isn't it?"

Lady jerked her head down, and clicked her tongue hard against the roof of her mouth. The devilish grin on the young woman leaning on the fence about ten feet up ahead mocked her. Her perfectly prim and proper ankle-length dress with all its lace and soft fabric moved around her legs in the light breeze. The woman kept grinning at her despite Lady's growing pout, face painted and lips red. Lady trotted up and shoved the girl in the shoulder, clacking together the pearls on her necklace.

"Agatha, you sly fox," Lady said. She crossed her arms over her chest, and straightened her shoulders back, relishing her two inches of height over the shorter woman. "What're you doing out here?"

"A little birdie told me that the famous Dragon Slayer of the Northern Falls was headed to my neck of the woods," Agatha said, rolling a strand of pearls around her index finger. She shrugged her shoulders in a cute bounce, and licked the side of her painted lip. "How could I not come out and greet one of my best customers as she came to town? You never visit!"

"Very easily," Lady said, walking past her. "And I'm hardly your best customer when it comes to buying gems, considering I only do it once in a blue moon."

"You still buy things," she said, pouting slightly. "That has to count toward your customer reputation somehow."

"You want something," Lady said, pointing over her shoulder. Agatha stepped away from the fence, her heels clacking on the cobblestone road. She tapped her way up next to Lady's side, pressing her fingers together and giving Lady the biggest set of puppy dog eyes her long eyelashes could manage on that heart-shaped face. Lady sighed, "What happened?"

"I'd playfully deny it, but as it stands my matter is rather serious. So yes, I do need something from you," Agatha said, stepping over a rock in the road. She laid one hand over the other, resting them neatly on her chest. Agatha always was one for dramatics. To further that image, she did this tiny sway of her hips as she walked that swished her thick skirt in the air as she attempted to look innocent. She even tipped her head up to look pitifully at the sky. Agatha said, "I may have have a bit of a theft problem."

"And how do I help with that?" Lady asked, shifting her pack and scrunching her nose. "I deal with beasts, not people."

"Which is why you are absolutely the right woman for the job." Agatha's smile turned crooked as she smiled up at Lady. "My thief is a dragon."

Agatha's manor towered over the rest of the buildings at the edge of the town proper, and was impossible to miss if you were approaching by the main road. With three stories, the top most floor was host to a balcony that ran around the full exterior of the building that offered a wonderful view of the area's famous vineyards. It was the sort of house nobility would have for their summer homes, but to sleepy little Vineyard Acres, it might as well have been a castle.

Lady sat in a plush chair in Agatha's main tea room, her bag resting on the floor next to her feet. She stretched out her legs and crossed them at the ankles as her host settled in across from her on the other side of the decorated tea table. Agatha snapped her fingers and a servant began serving tea in delicate porcelain cups, and preparing small square-shaped cakes with grapes made of frosting painted on the tops.

Lady shoved one of the treats into her mouth, and mumbled, "You have a dragon thief?"

"Yes!" Agatha threw her hands in the air, putting her entire body into the motion. Her thick skirt rustled with the movement, knocking up against the table. She picked up her tea cup and took an angry sip of the hot liquid, while her other hand grabbed the top of her skirt. Agatha slammed the cup down hard enough in its saucer to crack the plate. "And he's being damn sneaky about it!"

Lady swallowed a mouthful of tea and hummed as a man servant quickly swapped out Agatha's chipped flatware for a new, unblemished set. "Oh?"

Agatha leaned forward, setting her arms on the table with a scowl. Under the table, she stretched out her legs, crossing her ankles, and tapped her feet against Lady's shin armor. "He's not attacking in his dragon form! So no one believes me when I say I have a dragon robbing my jewelry stores blind!"

"How do you know it's a dragon and not, say, someone pretending?" Lady asked, spinning a tea cup around in her hand. She grabbed it by the base with her fingers through the handle and held it up to sip. "Dragons taking human form for information gathering is pretty common, but they almost never stay that way when they actually steal things for their hoards.

"Since they, you know," Lady said, tapping her finger against the base of her neck where most dragons kept their hoard sacks behind their scales. "Don't exactly have somewhere to put it all when they're human."

"I know that," Agatha said, pointing her finger square at Lady's chest. She pressed her lips together, smearing her perfectly applied lip color. Agatha nearly growled as she spoke, turning her blush covered cheeks a more impressive shade of pink. "Believe me. I've got a good, gut feeling about this. It's a dragon, and I want you to kill it and get my inventory back! I've got a living to maintain, you know!"

"I do," Lady said. She rubbed the side of her cheek hard, and leaned her head back on the chair. "You going to pay me, or is this just a favor? Because I'm not fond of doing freebies when the dragon isn't in the proximity attacking."

"Liar," Agatha said, tapping her own nose with the tip of her finger. She sat back in her chair, and crossed one leg over the other at the knee. "I happen to know you're quite the workaholic when it comes to the fine business of dragon slaying. All someone has to do is say the word 'dragon' and you go running to kill it, payment or not."

Lady narrowed her eyes, and gently set her cup back down on the table. "Are you keeping tabs on me?"

"What?" Agatha gasped, and held her chest with her hands. "Me? Never."

"Liar."

Agatha snorted, and smoothed her hair down. The curls bounced immediately back up, and she licked the side of her teeth. "Fair enough, but that doesn't change the subject: Are you going to help me, or not?"

Lady grabbed another cake, and shoved it in her mouth as she stood up and grabbed her bag. "What store is he hanging around?"

She hated that Agatha wasn't wrong.

"I knew you'd help!" Agatha said, running around the table and hugging Lady tight around the waist. She squeezed hard, smearing her make up against Lady's armor and rocked them both back and forth. Agatha released her hold after a full minute of delighted laughter and smacked both sides of Lady's waist playfully. "The main store in the center square. You can't miss it, believe me."

"We'll see," Lady said. She hitched her bag over her shoulder and sighed. "But I'm not going until tomorrow. Right now all I'm doing is finding a hotel to crash in."

Agatha gasped, and hit Lady in the side with her knuckles. "Don't be silly! You're working for me right now, which means you're staying right here in a guest room. Don't even bother to argue, I've already decided and had the best set up for you."

Lady looked around the current room, taking in the plush furnishings, the servants, and the plate still full of tea cakes. She smiled and shrugged, "Works for me."

Agatha was a ruthless, shrewd manipulator, but high heavens above did she have good taste in bedding.

Lady sunk a foot into the mattress the second her back hit it, and she could have stayed right there forever surrounded by silky sheets that were cool to the touch. Lady did love a good feather mattress when she could find one. There was going to be some catch to this whole dragon robber business, Lady was sure, but for right now this bed was the best place in the world.

She breathed in deep, inhaling the wonderful aroma of crushed and dried flower petals in a basket just to the left of her head on the night table. Lavender, vanilla, and just a hint of honeysuckle. Lady rolled over onto her side under the blankets, running her hand back and forth over the soft sheets. Luxury. This was luxury.

A flash of green eyes entered Lady's mind as she lay there, soft moonlight coming in through the window.

Lady rubbed the front of her eyelids with the base of her palm, and grunted. It figured thinking of luxury and riches would bring the self-proclaimed "spoiled noble" to mind. Days away in another town, and she was still thinking about Amadeus. The calm collection of his demeanor. The way his eyes lit up while staring at the ruby in his hand. That far too attractive laugh and perfect teeth.

He was impossible to get out of her mind.

Lady growled and rolled over onto her back, throwing her arms out at her sides. She couldn't possibly still be thinking of that man. She'd met plenty better in her days, both wealthy and not. Lady grabbed her sheets tight in her fists. He was just some bored man who stole rubies from dragon hoard guts. Lady rolled onto her stomach, and covered the back of her head with the far too soft pillow. She sunk into the mattress again as she shifted, and closed her eyes.

He was handsome, though.

Lady squeezed her eyes shut and counted to ten. She needed sleep. *Sleep.* Lady would get her rest and then handle Agatha's thievery problem. Once that was done, she would get moving on her way. Lady has spent years of her life training and mastering her skills. And it was time to move on to bigger and better things. Her journey was coming to an end with the Ruby Mines only another month's travel away.

This was the year that she'd kill the Obsidian of Ruby.

After that, Lady could finally concentrate on other things. Like starting a family of her own, or even going so far as to settle down in one place. Handsome faces might not be such a bother then. Lady relaxed into the bedding, her fingers playing with the edge of the pillow's case. Kill the dragon bothering Agatha and move on. That was the current plan, and Lady was going to stick to it.

By her father's birthday, she'd be back home with that dragon's head to lay on his grave and everything would be fine. But until then, there was no time for handsome men with green eyes in that plan.

None at all.

"Oh, you have got to be kidding," Lady said, walking into Agatha's main store.

Standing about ten feet in front of her, inspecting a case full of gemstone jewelry, was a man in silver armor with familiar black hair. Amadeus turned over his shoulder and smiled at her with glimmering teeth she was learning to hate, no matter how good they looked. Lady held her head up took a few steps into the store. What were the odds of running into him here?

Lady said, "Ama——"

"Amadeus of the Ruby Mines!" Agatha shouted, shoving Lady aside as she entered her own store right behind her. Lady smacked into the doorway as Agatha trotted over to Amadeus holding her skirt up to keep from tripping. She stopped a foot away from him, giving him a polite distance Lady had never seen Agatha display before, and clapped her hands together. "What an absolute treat! What has you here in my lovely shop?"

"I was passing through, and heard this was the place to be for the latest fashion styles," Amadeus said. He patted the top of her glass case with his gloved hand and bowed an inch. Agatha flushed, and Lady tapped her toe on the ground. Amadeus gestured to a heavily decorated gold necklace inlaid with rubies and sapphires. "Your store has become quite the trendsetter as of late, and I was curious where you were getting your gemstones."

"Oh, only the finest of mines and quarries, of course," Agatha said, pressing her hands into her chest. The white lace of her gloves didn't so much as wrinkle as she weaved her fingers together. Agatha took a step to the side, showing off a sparkly collection of red gems. "I'm sure you'll recognize a few of the stones from our ruby collection. There really is no place better than the Ruby Mines for those!"

"I know," Amadeus said, confidence oozing off him between his smile or the laughter in his eyes. "I make sure of it."

"Wait, wait," Lady said, pointing back and forth between Amadeus and Agatha. She stepped between them, and stared Agatha down as she pointed behind her. "You know this man?"

"Well of course I do," Agatha said, raising an eyebrow into the rim of her white bonnet. She glanced between the knowing smile on Amadeus' face, and Lady's own confused expression. "Amadeus of the First Family from the Ruby Mines is the world's leading expert in assessing the value of precious gemstones, and is in charge of all of their exports. He's invaluable to my business, but what I want to know is how you know him."

"We met in a fashion much like how you and I met so long ago, Miss Agatha," Amadeus said. He kissed the back of Agatha's knuckles, lingering for a moment before returning her hand. Agatha blushed redder than her lipstick, and Lady's flushed in what she viciously denied was jealousy. Amadeus motioned with his hand to mimic taking a swig. "Shared a drink or two."

"Oh, did you?" Agatha said, tilting her head just enough to the side that her bonnet rim covered one eye. The other twinkled in amusement. She pressed her lips together and rolled them in to pop them back out. "Why, Miss Lady! I didn't know you had it in you."

"We shared a drink, not a bed, Agatha," Lady hissed, desperately keeping the small hints of regret about that out of her voice. She smacked the merchant in the arm, and huffed. "Would you please behave yourself?"

"I didn't suggest anything of the sort!" Agatha shrugged. She shoved Lady back to the side, and stepped up closer to Amadeus. Agatha rubbed her hands together, almost wringing them in delight. "But enough of that, would you be interested in learning more about my wares and items? That is why you came, isn't it?"

"I would be delighted," Amadeus said. He turned to Lady and held out a hand toward her. "Would you care to join us?"

Lady swallowed, and remembered her plan. The "catch the thief and get out of town plan as soon as possible" plan. Amadeus continued to hold his hand out, palm up and waiting. There wasn't time for flirting in the plan. Lady shook her head, "No thank you. I have a job to get done for Miss Agatha and then I'll be moving on, I'm afraid."

"A job for Miss Agatha?" Amadeus asked. "May I ask what?"

"Nothing!" Agatha said, grabbing Lady's arm. Her death grip could have bent Lady's armor if she squeezed any tighter. "She's just teasing you. Could you please, just give us ladies a moment?"

Agatha dragged Lady out of the shop with the force of a wild bull, and shoved her out of view of the store front windows. Probably so Mr. Tall, Dark, and Handsome—Lady cursed at herself for even thinking of him that way—couldn't see their lips moving. Agatha, with strength Lady didn't know she had, pushed the dragon slayer up against the wall in the side alley of her store and blocked Lady's way out. Agatha gripped her hands into fists in the air, and then slowly opened her fingers and counted to ten.

"Lady, darling," she said, "that man, is the most prestigious authority in my field. He works for royalty!"

"Yes, I get it," Lady said, rolling her eyes. "He's a big deal. What has you so up in arms?"

"He can not know that I've been having theft problems, let alone dragon ones!" Agatha hissed. She knocked Lady in the chest with her knuckles. "So don't you dare say a peep about why you're here, or what you're hunting! Have some common sense in that head of yours!"

"Okay, okay," Lady said. She held her hands up defensively and rolled her eyes. Agatha continued to fume, and Lady zipped her lips across with her forefinger and thumb to appease the merchant. "Not a peep out of me."

"Thank you," Agatha breathed a sigh of relief. She held her chest with her gloved hand, and sucked in a slow breath before exhaling to calm herself. "This means more to me than you know."

"I promise not to ruin this for you," Lady said. She slapped Agatha lightly in the arm. "I'll come back later and look out for your dragon when Amadeus is long gone."

"Good," Agatha said, fixing her hat. She smoothed her dress down and touched Lady on the arm. She patted it twice, before heading back to the mouth of the alley. "Thank you."

Lady waved, as her friend wandered back around the corner and into her shop. She tugged lightly on her braid, before heading down the alley in the opposite direction. Lady would kill some time in a bar or something until the evening.

What were the chances of the dragon coming out in the middle of the day, anyway? It was still bright out!

Chapter 3

BUT WHILE THE ruby roses had decided on a course of action, it did however, take quite some time for the roses to decide what sort of company that they would like. Who would be best to admire them? What sort of company would be most appropriate?

Should they chose an animal? Maybe perhaps a dog or a cat to run about and play between their stems? Or maybe a small flock of ladybugs to rest on their shining petals? Honeybees were always pleasant, buzzing about and dancing in the air.

But none of those options were quite what they wanted.

After much discussion, however, the ruby roses of the fields decided they needed life with care and ability. Something that could do more than just appreciate their existence. The roses needed a creature that could write about them, that could speak brilliant words of praise.

They needed a human.

The harvest moon hung heavy in the sky, a brilliant orange glow on the horizon that bathed the town in its light. Mixed with the soft yellow light of the street lamps, one would think Vineyard Acres was more famous for oranges than grapes the way the warm hue accented the streets. The self imposed curfew of small towns and cities was well in effect, leaving the streets near empty. A drunk wandered here or there, but the "respectable" citizens had all long packed up for the night to be ready for a morning of work and shopping.

The perfect time to go dragon hunting.

Lady traveled light in the streets, having left her pack back at her room in Agatha's mansion with only her side bag and sword on her belt. Though she hated to admit it, it was nice having a safe place to keep her things while she worked. Inns were only so trustworthy these days, and when you lived where you walked, it could be hard keeping track of the essentials. But for now, she didn't need to worry and could stalk her prey freely without any extra burdens. Lady tapped on the cobblestones, eyes open for anything or anyone that seemed out of place in the quiet vineyard town.

Agatha's store was the biggest on the street, and as easy to spot in the night as it was during the day. It truly was the village's center piece: A giant made of stone and metal in the midst of tiny wooden houses and shop fronts. Lady wondered if it was irony that a jewelry store was the centerpiece of a place called "Vineyard Acres," supposedly famous for its grapes. But that was neither here nor there. What mattered, is that the building looked like a blinking beacon: The perfect target with its large glass bay windows shining under the moonlight. They practically glowed, shouting to anyone flying over head "Shiny things inside!"

Lady looked through the windows, the outsides glistening from the moonlight, but inside the store was pitch black past the slight leak of light from the street. She didn't see any movement in the shadows, and it looked untouched from when they locked everything up during the day. The front doors were still shut tight, and it looked as if nothing was disturbed there either.

She huffed, "I hope he shows up soon. I don't want to be here all night."

"Did you miss me that much?" A smooth voice asked from just over her shoulder.

She whipped her head to the side and found herself face to face with Amadeus, appearing almost out of no where in the dark streets. His eyes were playful in the night's light, and his teeth were showing through his smile. Lady shoved him away a good foot, and frowned. "I wasn't talking about you!"

"That job you said you had for Agatha, then?" Amadeus asked, looking into the shop. He held his hand up to shade the light, and browsed around with quick eyes. "She was rather hell bent on distracting me from the topic earlier, but I must admit I am curious. What could she need the help of a dragon slayer for, I wonder?"

"I wonder," Lady said. She turned and placed her back against the window pane, but careful not to lean on it lest her armor scratch it. Agatha might kill her if Lady somehow harmed her precious store. That woman could be scarier than any dragon when you got on her bad side. Lady watched the streets, for any sign of movement. Dragons didn't wait because you had company. "Did you have a nice evening?"

"The company could have been better, but I suppose Miss Agatha has her fine points," Amadeus said. He straightened away from the window, and smoothed his hand down his armor under the red traveling cloak. Lady watched him watching her from the corner of her eye. Amadeus rubbed the side of his cloak between his fingers. "It is a lovely night, isn't it?"

"It is," Lady said. A rat darted out from behind an alley way and scampered across the cobblestone. She held the side of her head and shook it. Lady turned to face Amadeus, and tried to sound as polite as possible. "As flattered as I am that you sought out my company, I'm afraid I'm working at the moment. So our little visit will have to wait for another time."

"If you insist," Amadeus said. He looked over her shoulder, and whistled lightly. "Looks like we have company, anyway."

"Oh god," a man said just from behind Lady. The cracked voice, and tremble of fear was audible in the two syllables.

Lady turned around and saw a young man in shredded clothing trembling violently, frozen in the middle of the street. Messy black hair was wild on his head, and his eyes were wide as saucers as he looked at the two people in armor standing before the store. Sweat beaded on his face, and he shook his head back and forth slowly in terrified disbelief.

"D-d-dragon!" He stuttered before cutting himself off, slapping his mouth shut hard enough to knock his teeth together.

The man turned and sprinted away hard on his heels like the devil was chasing him down in person.

"What on earth was that?" Lady asked the air, her hand on her sword.

"That is a good question." Amadeus leaned toward her, and spoke directly in her ear. "Why would a young man like that be so terrified of a dragon slayer?"

"Shit!" Lady said, and made a dash after him.

A man wouldn't be scared of a dragon slayer.

But a dragon sure as hell would.

31

Lady kept pace with the dragon as he ran, eyes glued on the terrified dashing figure just in front of her. She was determined to keep up the chase as long as it was, even if it took all night! How could she have been so out of it to not notice the disguise immediately? All the signs were there: beady eyes, torn clothes, the twitches! The illusion was so obvious now, Lady could just hit herself for not seeing it immediately.

Stupid, distracting Amadeus.

The disguised dragon kept going at a full blown sprint in the empty streets, moving at a speed no regular human could maintain. As much as Lady hated to admit it, the gap between them was growing by the second. It paused for only the briefest moment to knock over a stand behind it, spilling the packed up goods all ready for the morning market onto the cobblestone. As it turned, the dragon tripped over his unfamiliar feet and knocked over a barrel, stumbling as he tried to regain his pace.

"Stop now and it'll go easier on you!" Lady shouted, jumping over the barrel with ease. Her armor clattered together heavily as she moved, the rough and reliable plating sliding in and out of place never hindering her mobility. Lady drew her sword as she turned the corner, holding it at her side as she ran. "I'll get you either way!"

"Never!" the dragon shouted back over his shoulder. Not watching its front, the dragon missed the out of place stone brick jutting up from the ground. It yelped, tripping hard onto the street, and crawled on its elbows and knees until the dragon fumbled his way back up to its feet. Head forward, and fear driving, its sprint doubled. "I want to live!"

Lady cursed through her gritted teeth when the dragon started to roll its shoulders back and forth, turning and twisting its spine as the beast ran. Its skin molted, loose chunks of it moving and wriggling like something was trying to break free. Lady ran faster, her grip on her sword increasing. That little sneak was trying to transform mid-run!

The beast ripped its shirt off over his head with a clawed hand exposing its back. The skin peeled up in tiny sheets, revealing slick blue scales one by one on the dragon's form. It stumbled as the beast struggled to finish the transformation faster than it should normally take, its body pulling and tugging in various directions as its mass shifted in size.

Lady pushed her feet faster, shouting with all the venom she could muster, "Don't you dare!"

32

"Can't stop me," the dragon said, its voice hoarse and groaning. A half growl escaped the beast, and its voice morphed into a roar. "Not today!"

The wings sprout from its back spraying blood behind it as the fake skin ripped away in shreds, disintegrating into dust as it hit the ground. The dragon flapped his wings hard, lifting off the ground with at triumphant roar. With the transformation finished, all that remained was a small dragon dressed in blue scales.

"A Mini," Lady cursed under her breath. Miniature Dragons were the scavenging rodents of the dragon kingdom, small beasts no larger than horses that preyed on chickens and livestock. Most people didn't need the help of dragon slayers to take care of them, and the braver civilians even hunted them down to keep as trophy pets. The dragon flew up over the roofs, and Lady jumped on a stack of cargo crates to get up on the roofs and follow. She kept the glittering blue scales in her eyes as the slim figure flew faster. "Of course that's what's been bothering Agatha."

She jumped from building to building as she chased, but Lady ran out of rooftops before she caught up. She cursed, sliding to a stop on the final roof near the edge of town. A loose tile clattered out from under her foot on the roof's end, shattering on the ground below her. Lady dropped her sword back into its hilt, and turned around with a huff. She started on a long walk back to Agatha's store via the rooftops. The view was better up here anyway, and she doubted that dragon would be back anytime soon after a scare like that.

She hoped.

The only way to know for sure was to camp out here a few days at Agatha's mansion and keep watch on her store. Either the dragon would show up in a few days when it thought the coast was clear, or it would head on to another town where the dragon wouldn't be Lady's problem. She jumped down onto the street when she hit the main road, her armor clicking as she headed back to the store. Lady licked the side of her lip as she approached Agatha's building, her steps slowing as she arrived.

Amadeus was still there waiting for her.

He leaned on the wall, humming quietly to himself as he past the time in the moonlight. He polished his armor with the edge of his red cape, rather obsessed with making sure the armor remained pristine. The top of his black hair shined almost as bright as his armor, creating an almost halo glow around him. Lady pressed her lips together, and breathed in through her nose.

Lady stopped beside him, lightly punching his arm in the shoulder. "You must not have anything better to do if you spent your night waiting on little old me."

"You're hardly little, nor old," Amadeus said. He cracked an eye open and straightened up to turn fully to Lady. She looked up, and finally noticed after all this time that he was taller than her by a good four to five inches. Amadeus flicked her shoulder armor with his fingertip, a playful gesture that made her heart skip. "And it's hardly wasted time."

"You going to spend all of your time contradicting me, then?" Lady asked. She shifted to her other foot, and crossed her arms. Lady stared at the display case just past his elbow in the shop. "That's all you seem to be doing these days."

"Hardly accurate, since it's only been a few hours."

"See! There you go again," Lady said. She met his eyes, and pushed lightly on his chest through his cape. "I know for a fact you'll keep that up. I can feel it."

"Care to test it?" he asked.

"And how would we do that?" Lady returned.

Amadeus held out his elbow and bowed slightly. "Would you allow me the privilege of buying you a drink and a late dinner?"

"You could," Lady said, walking past him and leaving the elbow hanging in the air. No matter how tempting it was to take it. Lady held her head up. "If everything wasn't already closed at this hour."

"Then how about tomorrow?" he asked, looking hopeful as a puppy. It was rather unfitting on such a handsome face, and Lady hated for it to remain there. Amadeus asked, "Would that be better?"

"We'll see," Lady said, biting the edge of her lip.

"Then I bid you good night," Amadeus said. He tipped his head, and turned down the street toward the main inn down the road.

Lady watched him go, crossing her arms. *Was that the right choice?*

"You have to go out with him," Agatha said, leaning over the table to get into Lady's face. She gripped the sides of the tiny tea table with a death grip, the veins on her knuckles straining and visible through the gloves. Agatha got on one knee in her chair, to lean farther in to get next to Lady's cheek. "You like him anyway. I can tell. And it's important to make him happy, which would make me happy. So you have to go."

34

"I think you might be making too big of a deal about this, Agatha," Lady said, leaning back. She spread her legs out in front of her, slumping down into the chair. "I mean, sure he's handsome and a little witty—"

"Very witty. The man's a dream. You should date him," Agatha interjected.

"But," Lady said, gritting her teeth. "Even if I find him attractive, I don't have time for that sort of thing right now. I need to finish up here and then keep moving."

"Oh, for what!" Agatha said, sitting back and slouching into her chair. She smacked both of her hands into the fullest part of her skirt, making an audible "poof" from the impact. "Killing that famous dragon? You say you're ready and willing to go do it every other year, and start on your merry way there, but! But! You always get close and then turn around because you don't want to risk being unprepared. Why is this year any different?"

"That's precisely why this year is different!" Lady said, grabbing a cookie off the tray. "I'm tired of falling into the same trap. I'm ready. I'm ready this time."

Lady bit into the cookie, snapping off a piece with her teeth. "So no time for boys until after that monster is dead."

"It's not like you have to marry the man." Agatha rubbed the side of her temple, her chest breathing heavy in her aggravation. The lace on the top of her bosom stretched in and out with the movement. "You're hardly a saint, you know. You don't run around a lot, but you've done it. It wouldn't kill you to have a little fun."

"I know that!" Lady said, shoving the rest of the cookie into her mouth. "I just mean that for right now, I want to focus."

Agatha sat up and crossed one leg over the other under her overflowing skirt. The satin fabric shimmered from the morning sun streaming in through the window as it moved. She set the side of her chin in her hand, and hummed lightly. Lady shifted in her chair, as Agatha's piercing brown eyes stared into her soul through her skin.

A moment later, Agatha's lip quirked into a smirk and she licked the bottom of her lip.

"I get it now," Agatha said. She pressed her palms together, tapping her fingers lightly against each other. Lady didn't like the look that was stretching on her face. "It is all clear, and I understand completely."

"Understand what?" Lady said, regretting ever meeting this woman.

"And stop looking at me like that!"

"This one isn't just a handsome man, he's *handsome*, " Agatha said, drawing out the syllables on the last word like she was eating a piece of cake. She separated her hands, and laid one on her lap, and with the other traced the edge of the tea cup with her finger. Agatha made the innocent gesture as lewd as possible with only the look in her eyes. Lady was tempted to hit her. Agatha continued to molest the cup with abandon. "He's not a possible one night of fun, but a lifetime treat."

"I don't even know what you're yammering about right now," Lady said, shaking her head. She dragged her heels back under the chair, and stood. Lady shook her head, holding her hands up in defeat. "You're speaking nonsense."

"No! I'm right!" Agatha said, jumping up from her chair. She walked over to Lady, grinning like the devil. "You don't want a one night stand, because you're scared this one might be *the one* and then you'll want to give up the hunt for that awful dragon so you can stay with him!"

"I barely know him!" Lady said, holding her hands out. "I'm not thinking about anything but the fact I don't have time for flings right now!"

"Instinct is a powerful mistress, honey," Agatha said, holding her head up. She held her hands out, framing Lady's face with her fingers in a heart shape. "And it's written all over you. Trust me, Lady, I know what I'm seeing. You can tell it in your own gut that this one's special to you. You're just scared of confirming it."

"You read too many romance novels," Lady said. She backed up, and pointed her finger right at Agatha's smug face. "I'll admit he's attractive, but he's not husband material."

"So you say," Agatha shrugged. She bit the side of her thumb, still grinning like a fool who'd gotten a bag of candy. "But I just want you to know that you're the one who said the 'husband' word first, now aren't you?"

Lady didn't bother to answer, and stomped down the corridor of Agatha's mansion in escape. Amadeus was worth a fling. Nothing more. It didn't matter how good looking he was, or how witty or how charming. One night stands were all Lady had time for and if she got involved with him there would be more. So no dating. That was it! Lady would maybe run into him once or twice in her last few days here on the mission, but there would be no dinner, no dating, and no fling!

"I'm glad that you decided to join me," Amadeus said, sipping a glass of wine.

Lady smiled in response, the expression forced and awkward, clutching to her glass. If Agatha said so much as one word when she got back to the mansion, Lady would pack up and leave. No goodbyes, no nothing. Agatha could handle her own dragon problem. Lady forced a sip down from her own cup, and tried not to wince at the bitter taste.

Amadeus leaned back in his seat, the plush chair much more fitting for his looks and polished armor than a bar stool had ever been. Lady set her glass down, glancing around them. Her wry smile twitched as she said, "If I'd known you were taking me somewhere fancy, I would have dressed up a bit."

"I think we're fine the way we are," Amadeus said. He laced his fingers together on the table as the server brought them fresh bread and an appetizer salad. Lady plucked a miniature tomato off the top of the bed of lettuce and popped it in her mouth. Amadeus used his fork to blend dressing with the lettuce, tossing and turning the light food around on their plate. "It'd be a shame to visit the famous Vineyard Acres and not stop for a glass of wine, would it not?"

"A little pricey for my tastes," Lady said. "Give me a beer and a bowl of porridge any day."

"Well, you're not paying for it, so it shouldn't be a problem," Amadeus said, grinning behind his glass. He rubbed his thumb on the base of the cup, fingers wrapped around the rest of the stem. "Though I imagine you're fully capable of treating us both. Surely a dragon slayer is paid well for their troubles?"

"They are, and I am," Lady said, crossing her legs under the table. Her armor shifted with the movement, catching the eye of a nearby patron. Lady pulled over her salad and dug in, eating as quickly as possible without looking like a pig. The faster they ate, the sooner she could get out of here. Lady flushed, wishing desperately he'd told her where they were going before they left. Lady could have borrowed a dress or a proper blouse, or something! "I just prefer the cheaper options when it comes to travel. Less conspicuous."

"Of course," Amadeus said, spearing a crouton with his fork.

They ate quietly from that point. The sound of silverware clicking together against china plates filled the room, and Lady sighed inside. There had been less awkward conversation when she was drunk, or stealing his food. Amadeus looked up when the server returned to grab their empty plates, replacing them with thick steaks and a side of potatoes.

"Though," Lady said, speaking up for the first time in the past twenty minutes, "there are perks to paying a bit extra."

"Amen," Amadeus said.

He tugged over his plate and cut into the meat, dripping pink all over his plate. The raw inside was nearly fully red, and Lady whistled. She bit the edge of her lip, and was doubly happy she had caught the waiter's arm to whisper her preferences after Amadeus had ordered for them both. "Not a well done, guy, I take it?"

"Wouldn't dare ruin a steak that way, would you?" Amadeus said, taking a bite of the cut.

"You tell me," Lady said, slicing open her steak. She turned her plate to show off the inside of the cut, and giggled at Amadeus' blanched face. The brown insides didn't leave room for so much of a blush of pink.

Amadeus laughed, a hearty loving sound that she remembered very clearly from the bar. It was joyful, without a hint of mockery on his part. It was beautiful.

Lady's heart beat picked up, and she jerked her knife into the plate, cutting hard into the meat.

"Are you alright?" He asked, cutting out another square.

"I will be when you try this steak and take back your words," Lady said, stabbing a slice of it with her fork. She held it up and handed it over to him. "I dare you to tell me that's ruined."

Amadeus took the fork from her hand, and chuckled. "Challenge accepted."

Chapter 4

THE ROSES SOON discovered that creating a human was not like making more of their own. Despite their best efforts, every attempted ended in failure. In order to spare others the horrors that they had created, the roses vowed to dispose of the remains in secret. Unspeakable magics took place that day, and the roses buried the leftovers far beneath their roots.

The roses attempts were defeated, but they still wanted.

The ruby roses would need help with this plan, if they ever would have someone to love them. It wasn't as if they could uproot themselves and steal a child. They had to make one themselves!

Certainly someone would aid them?

Lady buried her face into the mattress, holding the pillow tight over her hair. Dinner had been fantastic. Better than fantastic. Their rough start had been chiseled into a perfect evening as soon as the steaks hit the table.

Amadeus was smart, handsome, kind, and rich. To top it all off, he had this underlying bit of cruel wit that made Lady's heart beat and a smile that made her knees quake. He was disgustingly perfect in every way. Lady hardly believed him to be real and wished both desperately that she had never met him and that she could see more of him at the same time.

Where the hell had this man been all her life?

And why was he showing up now when she didn't have time for him? She had a mission and a personal drive that herded her toward a rather large goal that didn't leave room for the domestic and dating. One night stands? Sure. Every once in a while was fine. A quick overnight romp, followed up with a nice "thank you" in the morning, and then move on. Lady growled. She couldn't picture Amadeus being a one-night stand sort of guy, no matter how much he looked the part or had been hoping for it earlier.

To make matters even worse, Agatha's thief hadn't made so much of a peep or show in town. It was like he had never even been there in the first place! Lady smashed her cheek into the mattress hard. There was no mistaking it: Lady had scared him away for good, and that meant she had absolutely nothing to distract her from Amadeus and his stupid, brilliant smile. The jerk who kept asking her out, or walking with her on her stake outs. Always present. Lady groaned, clutching the pillow harder between her fingers.

The pillow was ripped from the top of her head, and she rolled over hissing, "Agatha!"

"You can tell me I was right, later," Agatha said, grinning. Fully dressed, with her brown curls wrapped up on top of her head and her gloves on like always, Agatha was ready for the day. Her dress was an obnoxious petal pink with white lace on every edge that set Lady's teeth to grinding. "Right now, I'm here to save the day and give you some wonderful knowledge to save your mind from exploding with the revelation that you're in love."

"I'm not in love and you were only a little right," Lady said, sitting up. Her nightgown bunched at her waist, and she shoved it down to cover her legs. "Now what is it that you think I should know?"

"Mr. Amadeus is headed home after he picks out a few trinkets from my shop for his personal collection this afternoon," Agatha said. She walked over to the guest closet and threw open the doors with the same dramatic flair as if she were about to make a grand entrance into a party. Beyond the finely detailed double doors was a double rack full of extravagant and elegant dresses, complete with their accessories hanging on matching hangers. Agatha flipped through the dresses with the tips of her fingers and a whistle. "And where is it that you are headed?"

"The Ruby Mines?" Lady said, pulling the covers up slightly as Agatha flicked through dresses like a woman possessed, dragging some out and placing others back in. A few of them landed on the floor in bunches as she searched for who-knew-what tossing them about. "To get the

Obsidian of Ruby. You know that, Agatha."

"Yes, yes, I do," Agatha said, sticking her head into the closet. Her skirt swished back and forth as she searched, pushing and pulling at the expensive fabric. "But do enlighten me again, where is it that Mr. Amadeus is from again?"

"The Ruby…" Lady trailed off and smacked herself in the face. "Mines."

"Exactly!" Agatha said, turning around quickly. Her skirt flared around her and she had the most horrific smile on her face. She had her hands behind her back and Lady was sure the devil was in the room somewhere. "Which means that you have plenty of time to get to know Mr. Right and make progress on your little journey to kill things!"

"I hate you so much right now," Lady said.

Agatha hopped to sit on the edge of the bed and pulled out a beautiful green dress from behind her back. It was the same color as Amadeus' eyes, though it didn't shine as brightly. Agatha leaned back, and held the gown up against her chest. "But you will love me once I get you in this dress."

Lady couldn't say that Agatha had lied.

The dress was lovely. The color was just the right shade of emerald to be Lady's favorite color, Amadeus' brilliant eyes aside, and it had only two layers of the under skirt. So it was frilled and puffed out, but not overbearing or in her way when she walked. The top was sensible, with long sleeves, a v-neck on the second layer, and the under layer had a high collar that was edged with a thin line of lace and hid most of her burn scars. Lady felt naked without her armor, but even she could admit that this dress looked like it was made for her.

"Well, what do you think?" Agatha said, standing behind her. Her hands were on her hips, and she tilted her head to the side looking over her friend and occasional lackey. "I did good, didn't I?"

"Yes, you did well," Lady said. She hummed and turned from side to side, looking at her waist in the mirror. Lady ran a hand down the back of her thigh through the fabric. The dress hugged her curves almost too well. "Though I'm wondering how you just so happened to have a dress in my size."

"I'm prepared for all situations," Agatha said, checking her face in a compact. She smoothed down her eyebrows with the back of her finger. "Besides, you're only a size smaller than I am and that's one of my old dresses."

"This is old?" Lady said, scrunching her nose. She plucked at the dress, rubbing the pristine fabric between her fingers. "It doesn't even look like it's been worn!"

"I haven't worn it," Agatha said, licking the side of her lip. "Green's not my color."

"Then why'd you buy it?"

"Because I could," Agatha said, snapping her compact closed. "Just like you're going to go have a nice afternoon out with Amadeus and convince him that it's a good idea that you two travel together."

"I don't think this is a good idea," Lady said. She smoothed down her skirt, desperate to think of any excuse to get out of this or throw Agatha off her matchmaking track. Lady waved her fingers in the air, and hummed. "What if all he was looking for was a one night stand?"

"He wouldn't have you asked you out on a second date, or the third one, or the fourth," Agatha said, digging through a drawer in the nightstand. Finding what she wanted, she slammed it shut with her hip. Agatha reached up and put a flower pin in Lady's hair, just above the bulk of the braid on the scarred side of her face. "What do you think?"

"Whether or not my armor plating would fit over the dress."

Agatha smacked Lady in the arm.

Lady dug her fingers into the thickest part of her skirt. Her breath hitched, and she swallowed deeply trying to get rid of the knot lodged in her throat. Her heart felt like it was beating for two, and sweat beaded on her clammy skin. Lady shook her head and reached up to pat herself on the cheeks. She'd faced down dragons larger than city buildings. She'd gone toe-to-toe with some of the fiercest Medium and Large sized dragons their world could throw at her. Lady had survived an attack from the Obsidian of Ruby himself!

And yet a handsome man in silver armor standing on the other side of a piece of glass, harmless enough while browsing a jewelry case, is what made her knees quiver and her stomach clench.

How was that fair?

Agatha gave Lady a much needed shove, pushing her through the open door and stumbling toward the other man. Lady hissed behind her and waved away the meddling woman with the back of her hand. She picked up her skirt, and kept walking on her own.

Amadeus was already chuckling at her, watching with a glint of amusement in his eyes that made Lady want to smack him.

Or kiss him.

Lady's mind was a bit of a mess at the moment and she was going to drown in all out with alcohol later. And Agatha was going to pay for it!

"If I were to compliment you on the lovely dress, would it be welcome?" Amadeus asked, turning away from the jewelry case. His armor shined under a new coat of polish, and his red traveling cloak was once again tied around his shoulders. In the proper daylight, Lady could see that it was clasped together with a silver rose. Lady pressed her skirt down and seizing the opportunity, Amadeus took her hand and kissed the back. "It's hard to tell whether or not you enjoy wearing it."

"The dress is fine," Lady said, taking her hand back. She brushed her hair behind her ear, scratching there for a moment, before rubbing her hand down the back of her neck. "And a compliment from a gentlemen is always welcome when in good taste."

"Then allow me," Amadeus said, green eyes looking Lady over from head to toe. "You look lovely today, and that dress fits you well."

"Close enough," Lady said, forcing the lump in her throat to go down.

Amadeus straightened the top of his cape, nodding at the dress. "May I ask the occasion?"

"Agatha refused to let me leave town without dressing up at least once," Lady said, walking over to the nearest display cabinet. She placed both hands on the top of the glass and drummed her fingers as she looked down at all the little trinkets that caused such a fuss for humans and dragons alike. They were lovely, but Lady couldn't imagine killing anyone for them. "And since I get all of my bait from her, I ought to play nice."

"I'll have to thank her," Amadeus said. He walked around the cabinet, tracing his pinky finger along the glass. It glided silently, the smooth fine leather of his gloves sliding along like silk. Amadeus stopped at the last case and knocked his knuckles into the surface. "You think buying half her inventory would suffice?"

"I think you were going to do that anyway, and are using it as an excuse to flirt," Lady said, crossing her arms and walking around the side of the case to poke him properly in the chest. "Am I wrong?""

"I'd think that you were right," Amadeus laughed, the sound crystal clear like chiming glasses. He opened the case lid and picked up an emerald necklace, waving over an attendant to watch what he was doing. "Is there anything wrong with hitting two birds with one stone?"

"Not a thing," Lady said. Without her armor, she was much closer to his skin. Amadeus was warm, almost radiating a wonderful heat that made her insides melt. Lady leaned against his arm, looking at the gem he held. The small stone was surrounded by delicate swirls of metal shaped like vines. "Green really isn't your color, eyes aside."

"But it is yours," he answered. Amadeus turned, and placed the necklace around Lady's throat. It rested gently on her neckline as he clasped it in the back. Lady's nose nearly touched the front of his armor, and she held her breath. Amadeus' breath brushed her hair. "It really brings out the beautiful earth tones in your brown eyes."

"Flirt," Lady said, touching the tip of the gem.

"No more than you," he whispered in the side of her ear. Amadeus patted the side of her shoulder, and smiled. "Consider that a gift from me. A lady should have a few trinkets to herself, don't you think?"

"I don't know if I'd agree with that," Lady said, looking over her shoulder as he paid for a crate of gems and jewelry already packed nice and neat for travel. "But I won't turn it down."

"Wonderful," he said. Amadeus paid the nice man waiting on him, and ran his hand across the top of the crates as a young gentleman in a suit entered the store and grabbed the first box to carry out. Lady watched through the window as the young man place the box in the back trunk of a rather large carriage. He had blond hair, and she could see flecks of red shining on the lapel of his suit. Was he wearing a jeweled broach? Amadeus tapped Lady on the shoulder, drawing the attention back to himself. "Care to walk with me to my carriage? I would love to stay longer, but my travels are coming to a close with home calling so nearby."

"About that!" Lady said, holding up her hand to stop Amadeus from passing by. She cleared her throat and rubbed the back of her neck. "I was hoping to ask a little favor of you."

"Were you now?" Amadeus asked. He rested an elbow on one of the glass cabinets, and used his cape to polish a bit of the armor on his arm. He used his thumb through the fabric to buff out nothing as the blond came in and grabbed the next box for the carriage. "Whatever can I do to assist you?"

"As it turns out, you and I happen to have a similar destination," Lady said. She rubbed the side of her good cheek, and looked to the side to avoid his humor-filled smile. "And I thought it might be prudent to take advantage of that."

"You'd like a lift to the Ruby Mines, I take it?" Amadeus asked.

"Good guess," Lady said. She laced her fingers together, and leaned from one foot to the other. "Traveling by carriage is much quicker, and there's no sense in wasting such a good opportunity by not even asking, am I right?"

"Sound logic," Amadeus said, moving out of the way as the young blond carried out the last crate. When the path was clear, Amadeus walked by with his elbow held out for Lady to take. "How could I argue with it when my carriage is large enough to hold six, and yet seating only one? Such a waste, don't you think?"

Lady looked at the extended elbow, and then to his smiling face. She glanced aside, and saw Agatha leaning up against her storefront widows. She was mouthing "Take it!" into the glass and Lady covered her mouth with a giggle.

"I think you ought to do what your friend suggests," Amadeus said, leaning over and whispering in Lady's ear. "I'm sure it'll make her day."

"Hers or yours?" Lady asked, tapping the side of her burnt cheek.

Amadeus was dreadfully sincere and amused when he asked, "Can the answer be both?"

Lady couldn't say no to that face, with his uplifted eyebrows and shining smile. She hooked her arm through his elbow and hated how right it felt. "Only if you treat me to lunch before we're off."

"I think I can manage that."

Chapter 5

IN THE END, the ruby roses sought the help of a small fairy that had flown in through their fields. The tiny fairy was from the river, and through her many travels knew of magical creatures that may be able to aid the ruby fields in their search for a human to love them.

Specifically, she knew the name of a witch that lived on the far side of fields just beyond the mountain. The witch was famous for her potions and spells, and people came from miles around to seek her help and wisdom. If the roses sought her aid, there was no question that they could get what they wanted.

The fairy flew away after delivering her message, leaving the gemstone flowers with new purpose and determination.

"I think this carriage could double as a hotel," Lady said, pressing her hands into the plush seats. The fuzzy red fabric felt almost silky under her fingertips and undeniably soft. Lady's gloves and heavier armor rested on the floorboards near her feet leaning against the middle row of seating. "It's huge."

"Wealth has its perks," Amadeus said, sitting on the far side of the carriage. One leg was crossed over the other, and unlike Lady, he was still wearing all of his armor. Right in front of him, the inside had a fairly wide middle bench in the center that separated the seating on either side of the carriage against the walls. His traveling cape was draped over it, touching her armor gently as the carriage swayed from the ride. "I try to avoid flaunting it, but if there's anything to invest in, it's traveling well."

"I wouldn't disagree with that," Lady said, leaning back into the pillow that was sewn into the wall behind her head. The ride was smooth as they traveled down the roads, and she had to give it to the driver she'd met earlier: He knew how to handle the horses. Lady recognized him as the same young blond with the ruby broach who had been carrying crates out of Agatha's shop. Amadeus had introduced him as Drake, and said he was a personal manservant. Someone to wait on you who also knew how to drive? Lady didn't think it got much better than that. "This is the way to travel."

"Forgive me for asking, but is there a reason you've never invested in at least a horse? I would think your job included quite a bit of travel," Amadeus asked. He reached down to the floor, and pulled out a small box from under the seat. He set it in his lap, and opened it to reveal a bottle and glasses. Amadeus poured two drinks and handed one across the middle seats to Lady. "And I know that you should be able to afford that much."

"Afford the horse, yes," Lady said, sipping the wine. It was something sweet and light, almost like juice. "But that's not including the hassle of paying for its feeding, grooming, and of course the stable costs."

"I suppose those are concerns," Amadeus said. He sipped his drink slowly, watching Lady over the edge of the glass. "While I think I have a good guess about your reasons, may I ask what's bringing your travels to my Ruby Mines?"

"It's time to put things behind me," Lady said, leaning back and sipping the warm drink. The smell of it surrounded her, and her eyes dropped as she spoke. "Meeting you reminded me what I became a dragon slayer to do, and Agatha reminded me that I'm always putting off the final meeting. I'm always 'still training' or 'just one more kill under my belt', and never making any real progress."

Amadeus listened, swirling his wine around in his glass.

Lady stared at the rose imprint in his silver armor, and drank more of her glass. It was so much like her father's favorite shirt. If it hadn't had all those animals woven into it, it would have been identical. Amadeus had good taste in patterns. If he was that good at picking out armor, imagine what he could do with picking out dishes or clothes. How were nobles at domestic tasks? Lady swallowed the rest of her glass, drowning out the thoughts of domestic life.

She didn't have time to think on those things, not when the Obsidian of Ruby still breathed. Lady had to remind herself again and again lately it seemed.

"I'm ready for all this to be over," Lady said finally. She reached over and dropped the empty glass lightly into the box it had come from, and smacked the seat in the middle. "Dragon slaying is a rush like no other, and it keeps me fed, but I can't do this job forever, and I can't stop until that Great Dragon is dead."

"You do know that Great Dragons are called 'great' for a reason, don't you?" Amadeus said, handing his glass over to Lady. She took it and cradled the still full stemware between her fingers. "They are powerful, and not easy to kill, even for someone with your skill and talent. You may never be ready to fight him."

"Great Dragons bleed just like any other living creature on this earth, and they can die," Lady said, squeezing the stem of the glass. "I've trained my entire life for this, and I'll never be more ready than I am right now."

"Just promise you won't rush into things," Amadeus said, getting up. He stepped around the middle row, and sat next to her. Amadeus took the cup back from her and drank. "We've got a long way to go until we're home, and you have plenty of time to think things over."

Lady leaned against him, eyes drooping with the mixture of warmth from the drink and his shoulder. "I'm sure. Now is the right time, I can feel it in my gut."

Amadeus didn't answer.

Lady dropped her bag next to her bed at the inn. Amadeus paid for his travel in style, but he was modest with lodging. It seems their first meeting in that mid-priced inn was normal for him, only this time he sprung for the one of the better suites in the building with two beds, instead of smaller room with one. Lady stretched her arms high over her head, and looked down at the set of beds. A courtesy screen split the room, placing one bed on each side of the room.

But there was still no mistaking it: With Drake opting to stay with the carriage overnight to protect the precious cargo in the trunk, Amadeus had only rented one room for the both of them.

Lady tried to keep her heartbeat in check when she considered the multitude of things *that* could mean.

"Have you settled in yet?" Amadeus asked, popping his head in through the door frame. "The gardens here in Honey Farms may not be as lovely as the ones in Vineyard Acres, but their namesake honey that comes from the one down the street is to die for. It's like liquid gold, and twice as valuable. I was hoping we might share 'a spread of it on some bread' as the advertisement put it."

"You're quite the tourist, aren't you?" Lady asked. She sat on the edge of the bed, and leaned back, crossing her ankles. "I thought we were only stopping in for a rest?"

"Never pass up an opportunity when it's there, my dear," Amadeus said, with a twinkle in his eye. "Especially when it comes to good food."

Lady rubbed the side of her mouth. "I suppose it couldn't hurt."

"Wonderful," Amadeus said.

He wasted no time in taking Lady by the elbow and escorting her out of the room. Amadeus let go of her before they hit the stairs, and she wasn't sure if she liked that or not, but at least no one stared too much when the pair in armor hit the main floor. Amadeus paid for two drinks in bottles to go at the bar, and Lady enjoyed the gifted sweet water on their way to the tourist trap.

The walk to the garden was pleasant, though not as much as the honey they served in the garden café.

Lady moaned biting into the thick honey that was lathered over the freshly baked croissant. She rubbed the drippings of the thick syrup off the side of her mouth with a thumb, and licked it to savor every bite. "This is amazing."

"A worthwhile detour?" Amadeus asked, spreading butter onto a roll. Not a single crumb hit the table whether he was lathering it with the spread, or biting into it with his perfect teeth. "You were so eager to keep moving, I'm hoping that you'll forgive the lost time."

"Most definitely," Lady said. She pointed at the basket and then back at Amadeus. "We are taking a basket of these back to the room."

Amadeus nodded, and placed his bread back on the plate. He held it, keeping his fingers away from the melting butter threatening to run off the sides. Lady took another bite of her croissant, and frowned slightly. Amadeus tapped his finger on the counter. "I was thinking about what we discussed in the carriage this morning."

"Were you?" Lady asked. She reached over and grabbed his roll out of his hand, and took a bite of it. "I would have thought the matter was rather settled."

"In so much as that you're determined to kill that dragon," Amadeus said. He reached over and grabbed her wrist and pulled it back. He retrieved his roll, and ripped off a piece from the end she didn't bite from. He dipped it in a glob of honey on his plate, and popped it into his mouth. Even with the casual movement, not a drop of honey or crumb on the table. "But I still think that you're making a foolish decision."

"Your lack of faith is noted," Lady said, throwing her arm over the back of her chair. She almost put her boot on the table, but remembered that they were in public catching sight of the couple sitting at the table next to theirs. Instead, she shrugged heavily, and threw her hand up. I'm still doing it."

"Then how about this," Amadeus said, "why not get some practice in first?"

Lady laughed, and reached over for the jar of honey on the table. She picked up a spoon and ate it straight out of the jar. A drop of it fell on her armor and she scraped it up with the side of her hand. She licked the excess honey off her hand. "That sums up my profession, if you ask me. All I do is practice for that moment."

"Ah, but you mostly kill Miniature and Large Dragons," Amadeus said. He pulled off another piece of bread and ate it. "How many Great Dragons have you slaughtered?"

"I already told you that I haven't killed any," Lady said. She shoved another spoonful of honey into her mouth. "They aren't exactly as plentiful as their much smaller cohorts."

"So what if I told you that I knew where one might be?" Amadeus asked. He ripped off another piece of his roll and stirred it in the honey on his plate. "That isn't the particular one you're so eager to find."

Lady pulled the spoon down. "Do you?"

"A rather small one for the breed," Amadeus continued. Lady put the jar of honey back on the table, and scooted her chair closer to the table. Amadeus said, "If you can't take him on, there's no chance that you could take on your Obsidian of Ruby."

"And why do you happen to know that information?" Lady asked. She leaned over the table, and poked him in the chest. "It seems rather suspicious, if you ask me."

"Or maybe I'm just well informed, and didn't really need this information until I met a rather determined dragon slayer." Amadeus asked, "Are you interested or not?"

"Very," Lady answered, leaning forward across the table.

The Great Dragon's name was "Heart of the Drowned Lake", or "Lake Dragon" for people who didn't care to say his full title every time. While not as bloodthirsty as the Obsidian of Ruby, it was still the scourge of the area and attacked local villages on a regular basis because of their refusal to send tributes and general stubbornness. It was something that Lady admired, even if it cost them from time to time.

While the dragon could fly, it had taken up its home deep under a marsh underground. Instead of fire, its attacks were horrific blasts of scalding hot water that burned almost as badly, cooking people alive in a bath of water and steam. Everything else about it, however, was rather normal for a dragon, including the same weak point on the back of its neck. It was nice to know that even Great Dragons shared weaknesses with their kin.

Lady knew everything about him at this point through various questioning and interrogations of her companion, except for where the Lake Dragon was located and what his scales were made from. Amadeus was withholding that information until he knew for certain Lady wasn't planning to run off alone without him. Which of course was ridiculous! It was one thing for him to stand by and watch her take out a wyvern, but a Great Dragon?

"You are absolutely not going with me," Lady said, standing in front of Amadeus as he sat on his own bed. He crossed his legs, and looked perfectly content to let Lady rant even though his mind appeared to be already made up. "You'll be a liability and if it's as tough a fight as you keep hinting it will be, then there's no way I'll be able to fight him and look out for you."

"I can take care of myself," Amadeus said.

He leaned back, looking up at Lady's frowning face. His armor was laid out behind him on a chair, and he looked almost naked with only his undershirt exposed. Lady pouted harder, stretching the healthy skin against the glossy scarring. Amadeus was slim, with only the slightest of muscle on his form. Flawless skin and a delicate physique both attested to his lack of action and battle more than his shining armor would. He looked like a porcelain figurine that Lady's grandmother used to keep in her curio cabinet. A dragon would rip him apart if it ever got a hold of him. Lady crossed her arms, and straightened her back. She would not let that happen.

Amadeus rubbed his mouth, his hand attempting to hide the smile that was threatening to break free. Lady wondered if he was taking this seriously when his eyes held that much amusement. Amadeus held his hand up and shrugged. "I know how to stay out of the way."

"There's no need for you to be there," Lady said, poking him in the chest. "None at all."

"How about just being there in case you really are in over your head?" Amadeus asked. He took her hand and pulled out her crossed arms. Amadeus rubbed his thumb on the back of her knuckles. "I think I can handle grabbing you and running if it comes to that."

"Now who's overestimating himself?" Lady said, pulling her hand out of his grip and throwing her arms into the air. She held both sides of her head and breathed out. "Never mind. You know what? We'll talk about this in the morning."

"If you like," Amadeus said. He leaned down, pulling off his boots one at a time. He set each one neatly down on the ground next to the side of his bed. Amadeus folded back his covers with a quick flick of his hand. "We'll have plenty of time to chat in the carriage, considering the dragon is still a good two or three days travel away."

"Plenty of time to convince you to wait at the inn," Lady said, pulling off her armor and dumping it on the ground in a heap. She reached to change her undershirt out for her nightgown, but in an unfamiliar flash of bashfulness, left it on. For some reason, green eyes watching made her cheeks heat, and she was almost terrified to reveal a peak at even her backside. Lady tugged her blankets back in a bunch, slipping her shoes off with her feet alone. "Got it."

Lady slipped under her own covers and reached over to pinch out the candle lighting the room. Amadeus was already resting quietly on his pillow, the screen folded up at the front of the room. For a few seconds, Lady considered pulling it back out and separating the two of them for the night. She rolled over on her side, facing him and changed her mind.

Amadeus' eyes were shut and his mouth was slightly open to allow a slight breath in and out. Handsome awake, and handsome when he slept. How was that fair? Lady clutched tight to her sheets, and buried her face into the pillow. There was more to Amadeus than she was seeing. There had to be more to him than a pretty face and calm, witty demeanor. His chest rose and fell in even movements, relaxed and calm. Lady wanted to know him. The real Amadeus who laughed at her well done steaks, and not just the polite acquaintance she was getting to see now.

And she couldn't do that if he was murdered by a dragon.

Lady pulled her covers up, and held them close to her chin. She fell asleep watching him breathe.

Chapter 6

TO GREET THE witch, the ruby roses would need to travel. The old magic user lived far away, and the roses were bound in place to the earth by their stems. Should they be plucked, they would die. Such a fate was the inevitable for a flower. But to be worshiped was something they valued and wanted far more than life, so a sacrifice was needed.

A young volunteer, a budding rose no more a season old, agreed to have his stem split from the ground, and would travel with a passing bird to the witch's home. Like any normal flower plucked, his life would last a few days, maybe a week if he were blessed, before he was lost to the beyond.

That would be just enough time to ask for the witch's assistance, and leaving his dead, but still beautiful, corpse as payment.

There would be no price too high for this.

The Lake Dragon would have to wait.

Lady stood in the center square of Honey Farms with Amadeus by her side, both staring at a man in full armor wielding a sizable lance. The helmet covered his face, but it wasn't hard to see what his profession might be between the armor and the decorations of dead dragons embedded in the steel: A fellow dragon slayer. The sight wouldn't have been too out of place, considering there were quite a few people who shared Lady's job of choice, but the same could not be said for his steed:

A Miniature Dragon.

A large crowd of people had gathered around him as his dragon landed. Lady whistled at saddle on the beast's back, which extended along the neck in shifting armor plates to cover the dragon's weak point. A bridle sealed the Mini's mouth shut, the bit and straps of the restraints highly decorated and carefully engraved to match the slayer's armor. The dragon paced around on its four legs, disgruntled and not too fond of the man seated on his back if the way it glared or tugged at the controlling reins were any indications.

It was rather big for a Mini, about twice the size of a regular sized horse, but still no where near its Large sized brethren. The dragon's scales were made of brilliant rubies, shining red and glittering in the sun, and the smooth membranes of the underside of its wings shimmered in a rust color.

"People of Honey Farms," the man said in a bright and booming voice, muffled by the face mask covering his mouth and eyes. "I am Nicholas of the Razor Plateau. Do not fear, for this gorgeous little beastie is under my total control."

"As long as it's wearing the reins and bridle, right?" Lady asked, pushing her way through the crowd. She should have guessed he was from the Plateaus the second he landed. That area was swarming with Minis to the point that dragon riders were fairly common, or at least the area bred the ones with the most bravado. "How well behaved is it when your Mini isn't contained?"

"Rather well," Nicholas said, sliding off the saddle and standing next to the beast. He patted the side of its neck, and smoothed the hard scales down with wide, almost loving strokes. "And *she* has been very good to me."

The dragon jerked hard, and made a loud whine through the bridle bit that sounded like a roar desperate to get out. Nicholas turned and tugged hard on the reins. "What's the matter with you, now?"

"I'm fairly certain that dragon would eat you should she ever get free," Amadeus said, standing just behind Lady's shoulder. "It's their nature, you know."

"Nonsense," Nicholas shouted over his shoulder as he struggled with the increasingly agitated beast tugging back and forth as it tried to free itself from his hold. Nicholas yanked hard, stilling the dragon from all movement but its heaving breath. He shoved up the visor on his helmet, revealing bright brown eyes tinted with a hint of grey. "Maim and kill maybe, but she would never be so barbaric as to eat me."

Amadeus held up his finger to his lips and made a soft 'shh' sound, and shook his head. He kept his eyes on the dragon, even though he was addressing Nicholas. Lady bit her lip in amusement, watching the fancy little noble try and order around the fighter. "Shush now, or you'll lose your head over it won't you? It's never good to act on things you don't understand, now is it?"

"You're an odd man," Nicholas said, still rubbing the dragon's side. His massage of its glittering scales seemed to do the trick, and the dragon calmed fully after a few seconds. Its glaring continued however, the gaze intense as the dragon looked between Lady and Amadeus. Not sharing his dragon's wariness, Nicholas turned to Lady and smiled, grip on the reins still tight. "But you, I know! Lady of the Northern Falls, correct? You have quite the reputation!"

"I wish I could say the same of you," Lady said. She tapped the side of her burnt cheek, grinning side. "I do wonder what gave me away."

"It was your armor, actually. Not many slayers let their protection get into such disrepair." Nicholas laughed, a hearty, heavy sound. "A burn scar is hardly enough to identify a dragon slayer, considering our business."

"Fair point." Lady bit her lip and smiled. That was a nice cover up, considering that her scar was what Lady was famous for. As far she knew, Lady was the only woman dragon slayer with half her face burned in the general area. *Cute.* Lady trotted over to pat the dragon on the nuzzle, receiving a hiss for her efforts. "And what brings you here to frighten the nice people of Honey Acres?"

Nicholas tugged off his helmet, revealing a head full of nutmeg brown hair. It was loosely curled, and hung down near his neck in bouncing waves. His brown eyes were warm and lively in the full light, and his skin a healthy dark tan. "A quick stop for food and rest, before continuing East."

"And what's to the East?" Lady asked, despite herself. Amadeus inspected the tips of his gloves behind her, and she didn't need to turn to know he was already rolling his eyes at the two of them.

"A dragon, of course!" Nicholas said, nearly shining with the force of his smile. He put his helmet up on the saddle's side pack, and held his arms out. "A rather large dragon seems to be pestering the kind people of South River. A cousin of mine sent me a letter asking for assistance in slaying the monster, so how could I do anything but answer his plea?"

"South River? That's rather close," Lady said. The people that had milled about to see the dragon were slowly filtering away as they realized the Mini Dragon had given up its escape attempts and business became the topic. "I'm surprised we haven't heard anything about it here."

"The attacks are sparse," Nicholas said. He pushed on his dragon's neck again, and the Mini sat on its back haunches. It followed the motion through and laid down on its front with a yawn trying to escape the bridle. It huffed out a smokey breath as the dragon curled up on the street, the beast's tail sliding forward to rest around the slayer's feet. Nicholas leaned on his dragon's side, holding up a hand as he explained. "Usually he only attacks once every so few weeks, or in other words once a month at most. But the dragon has been silent for some time now, close to three months. They've seen bursts of fire coming from far over the hills, so they fear a large strike from the monster in the upcoming days."

"Ah, so you're going to cut it off before it gets the chance," Lady said. She tapped her boot toe behind her on the stone, and shot the visitor a cheeky grin. "I understand that correctly?"

"You've got it!" Nicholas chuckled, warm and bright as a summer evening. He gasped, his eyes open wide, and he snapped his fingers. Nicholas pointed at Lady with a grand smile, and a chipper question. "Hey, you wouldn't want to join me, would you? It's been a while since I had a good team up, and if he's as big as my cousin says, the help would be much appreciated from someone of your fame."

Amadeus coughed into his hand, and walked forward. Carefully placing himself between Lady and Nicholas, he dropped a hand on Nicholas' shoulder, shaking his head. "I'm afraid that's quite impossible since we're already on our way somewhere else."

"Now, wait just a minute," Lady said. She pointed at Nicholas and waved between him and his dragon pet. "If he needs help, I plan to give it. It's my duty as a dragon slayer, and I can always catch up with you later. We don't have to travel together the entire trip."

Amadeus sighed heavily, and rolled his eyes, clearly disagreeing with her. Lady ignored how that made the butterflies jump in her stomach. He released Nicholas' shoulder, and smoothed down his slick black hair. "You're a rather stubborn woman, you know that?"

"Is that a problem?" Lady asked, crossing her arms.

"I wish it were, sometimes," Amadeus said, a smile tugging on his lips despite the defeat. He turned, his cape flapping in the wind. "I'll go renew our hotel room for another night."

"He's rather gloomy, isn't he?" Nicholas whispered into Lady's ear.

"Only sometimes," she said, not bothering to cover her victorious smile.

Lady awoke in the middle of the night to find the bed next to her empty. She put her bare feet on the floor, and shifted to adjust her clothes. Lady rubbed the side of her eyes as she yawned, blinking blearily at the clock to double check the late hour. She stood, and looked about the room to see if perhaps he was just around the corner with the wash sink. "Amadeus?"

He wasn't there.

Lady picked up a coat from the chair and slipped on her shoes. Where did he go? She knew he was angry earlier about having dinner with Nicholas, but Lady couldn't help but think the jealousy was cute. She took great joy in watching Amadeus' upper eyebrow twitch every time she shoved or elbowed Nicholas in a friendly manner. Maybe Lady had gone too far? No, that wasn't right. His things were still there, including his armor neatly stacked by the floor. Amadeus wouldn't have left without those.

"He probably went to check up on Drake," Lady said to herself. She crossed her arms over her chest, yawning widely as she left the room. No matter how much Amadeus played up the master-servant role between the two of them, Lady could tell Amadeus and he were odd friends. Lady rubbed her arms as she descended the creaking stairs. "Poor man's been stuck with the carriage for two days now."

Lady stepped down into the main lobby of the inn, the entire building otherwise quiet in the dark of the night. Even the bar in the front serving area had closed up and kicked the last of the drunks to their rooms or the streets. The sweet smell of honey mead and butter lingered in the pub as she walked through it. As pleasant as that was, Amadeus wasn't down here, either.

Lady did find him, however, just outside of the inn near the back stables. Though instead of checking up on his carriage and manservant friend, Amadeus stood in front of the red dragon that Nicholas had rode into town, looking intently at something in his hand. The dragon itself was a bulky form that rested against the wall of the stable, far too big to fit inside any of its stalls. There was a tarp crudely hung over the beast, attached with rope to the alley walls. It breathed slowly, deep asleep under the shoddy tent.

Martha, Lady reminded herself: The dragon's name was Martha. Lady rubbed the side of her face. And Martha was a "she" and not an "it," as Nicholas was so keen to remind Lady. She really needed to get better about that before Nicholas' corrections stopped being so friendly. But that didn't matter right now, since both she and Amadeus should be taking notes from Martha and getting their rest!

"Admiring the dragon?" Lady whispered, as to not wake the beast. She adjusted the flimsy coat over her nightgown in the cold air. "Though that's an odd thing to do in the middle of the night."

"Not admiring so much, as inspecting," Amadeus said, holding up a scale toward the dimly lit lantern overtop the stable doors. He turned it over in his hand, letting the light reflect off of it in tiny, blinding shimmers. "It's always interesting to see these gemstones grow straight from the flesh of a living creature, when normally they're formed from deep within the earth. It makes you think about the wonders of our world, and I can't help but want to compare the quality."

"Did you rip that off?" Lady hissed, not nearly as impressed with the smooth stone. She smacked him in the side, happy to hear the slight sound of a slap without his armor to protect him. Lady pointed at the scale. "I know you like rubies, but that's a bit much. Don't you have an entire mine full of them?"

"Mine*s* with an 's', as in plural. I have quite a few ruby mines, but that's not the point." Amadeus shook his head and placed the scale-shaped gem in her hand. It was firm, and perfectly formed in the shape of a rounded diamond, as if cut and then smoothed down by a professional. "Scales fall off all the time. The rather plump Martha rolled over and scratched it—*No*, *"her!"*—herself in her sleep. As if to prove Amadeus' point, a handful of scales fell off her side during the shift, free for the taking. "I'm surprised there was even one left on the ground with the beggars snatching all the loose ones up the moment they fall."

Amadeus continued to talk, easy conversation in the dim lights about the wealth of dragon scales and how even weak men can grow brave when there's easy money to be had. But she had stopped listening.

Lady remembered a very different breed of shedding scales: Black glass falling from the sky, shredding everything in its path. Obsidian scales as sharp as knives, that exploded like shrapnel when they shattered on impact.

She sucked in a breath and handed the smooth stone back to Amadeus, practically shoving the thing back into his palm. Lady tucked her hair behind her ear, and turned away from the sleeping Martha and her blunt, harmless scales. "I suppose that's the truth. Sometimes I forget they drop things of value in their torment."

"Are you alright?" Amadeus asked, rubbing the side of the scale with the center of his thumb. The dragon next to them breathed heavily, letting small wisps of smoke escape the nostrils from her snout. "You look like you've seen a ghost."

"Just a bad memory." Lady smiled, looking over her shoulder. She licked her lips and rubbed her burnt cheek. "Not all dragons drop things as harmless as gemstones, do they?"

"No, they do not," Amadeus said, his eyes softening. Amadeus shoved the ruby scale in his pocket, and tugged her arm lightly at the elbow. "Come on. I've already disturbed your sleep enough with my midnight wanderings. Let's go back inside where it's warm."

Lady nodded, and felt free to lean on his side. For once, she was glad her and his armor were both off and upstairs. She could feel the heat of his skin through the shirt, and it served well as a center point to block out bad memories. Lady refused to focus on them any longer, not when she had the perfect source for new memories right here on her arm.

"Martha! My sweet Martha!" Nicholas exclaimed, throwing his arms open wide. "Who's my good girl?"

Lady laughed to herself as he hugged the side of his dragon's head, and let go just as quickly when Martha growled. Running his fingers up the length of her top horn, Nicholas then dropped to the second that was just below it to squeeze and slightly nudge it like a friendly pet. Martha had four horns at the back of her long head just behind two stout ears. The first two on the top were large and winding with small branches like a deer's, and the second two just under it were slightly curved like a goat's. It was a mismatched set that looked just plain odd on the beast.

Nicholas continued to coo at his monster as he saddled her up for the trip out to South River. He hummed as he worked, and Lady covered her mouth to stop the laugh. Nicholas rubbed Martha's side. "Who's going to be a good girl today with company? It'll be you, won't it?"

Martha responded to the childish, happy talk by smacking him in the side with her wing.

He fell on his backside, the armor clattering with him in a heap. Nicholas pulled himself up grabbing onto the side of her wing and tugged hard on her reins. "Must you always be so fickle, you?"

Nicholas went back and forth so often between the lovey-dovey talk and the frustrated scolding that Lady was beginning to wonder which was truth and which the act. But she supposed it was none of her concern as long as it didn't affect his performance.

Lady nodded toward Martha and asked, "Will you be riding her while we're in the battle, or is Miss Martha merely transportation."

"Of course she'll be joining me!" Nicholas exclaimed. He rubbed Martha's side, and shook it a bit to knock loose a few scales. He kicked them aside with his foot, and went back to adjusting her saddle. "Martha would never want to be left out of the action. Dragons may hate humans, but they're not too fond of each other, either. She's more than happy to help out."

"I guess that's true," Lady said, tapping her chin. "Can't say I've seen many dragons living together, or working together in my time. Save for Twins, but those are fairly rare."

"I think it's because of their greed," Nicholas said, straightening out the saddle blanket under the heavy leather portion of the seat. The pattern of the fabric was rather lovely, with weaving Forget-Me-Nots and strawberries. Rather sweet for a fierce slayer, but at least the lance that he hooked onto the side looked frightening. Nicholas asked, "Can you think of a dragon who'd be willing to share his hoard?"

"Can't say that I can," Lady said. She crossed her arms and leaned against the stable wall. Martha glared at her through the corner of her slit eyes, the ominous yellow glowing bright in the dim light under Nicholas' tarp. Lady looked to the alley, and adjusted her pack at her side. "They really are horrid beasts."

Nicholas cleared his throat, whistling a short tune. "So where's your grumpy traveling companion? I thought he was going to join us?"

"Amadeus?" Lady asked. She rubbed her arm and leaned forward to look in the stable. Amadeus' two horses were still nice and neat in their pens, ready to be hooked up to the carriage at a moment's notice. She didn't know where Amadeus was, but there was at least one person who ought to be keeping tabs on the man. Lady called over to the manservant who had taken to leaning quietly against a stable wall with his eyes shut. "Hey, Drake! Where's our favorite nobleman?"

Drake cracked an eye open, and answered quietly, "He said he was going to get something before we left, and I imagine he should be meeting us here any moment now."

"Irresponsible man, not even telling his servant where he's going," Lady said, putting her hands on her hips. "I really ought to give him an earful when he gets back."

"The nobleman is Amadeus, yes?" Nicholas asked, glancing at Drake. He rested his arms on Martha's back, leaning on her like she was a giant pillow. Finding that Drake wasn't in the chatting mood, Nicholas turned the rest of his conversation toward Lady. "I wasn't paying quite as much attention when he introduced himself at dinner as I should have."

"Yes, that's his name," Lady said. "And yes, he's First Family."

"Fancy," Nicholas whistled. He propped his chin up on both of his hands. "You don't see many of them mingling about with the rest of us, do you? Speaking, what has him as your traveling companion? Is he your financier?"

"Oh, no!" Lady said, shaking her hand in the air. She chuckled and ran a hand threw her loose hair, having yet to tie it back today. "Nothing like that. We're merely going in the same direction, and Amadeus happens to have a carriage when I have no horse."

"Ah!" Nicholas said. "Traveling companions! Those are a nice thing to have, you know. I rather regret that I'll be flying overhead instead of enjoying your company down below."

"You won't be missing much," Lady confessed. "The seats are comfortable enough that I must admit that I spend most of the ride napping."

"The joys of a rich traveling companion," Nicholas said, raising an eyebrow. "Even better."

"It's not like that, either," Lady scolded. She tapped her finger lightly on her armor's arm, watching the entry of the alley for any sign of his black hair and silver armor. "Though I do wonder what's taking him so long to get here."

Lady bit the side of her thumb. "I do hope he's alright."

"I'm sure he's fine." Nicholas put a hand on her shoulder and pushed lightly in a comforting gesture. He pointed to Drake, who once again looked to be napping against the wall, and said, "If the man in charge of his care isn't worried, I highly doubt that we need to be."

"I'm still going to scold him," Lady said, laughing and shoving Nicholas in the arm.

"No disagreement there!" Nicholas answered, making Lady laugh harder.

Amadeus arrived an hour later, bearing a bag of honey drenched butter croissants and a sincere apology for his tardiness. He was a wise man, distracting Lady from her anger with the nectar of heaven that was bread and honey.

Lady shoved a mouthful of the delicious treat into her mouth, asking around the bite "Where were you?"

"Visiting with local merchants," Amadeus said, directing Drake to pick up Lady's bag and place it in the storage trunk on the back of the carriage. When he had finished placing their bags among the crates of jewelry Amadeus had bought from Agatha, Drake closed it with a sound click and climbed up into the driver's seat. Amadeus rubbed a minuscule drop of water from his armor with his thumb. "I was hoping to find a contact in South River we might impose upon. I'd hate to put the burden of three people on Nicholas' relative."

"I already told you it's no trouble," Nicholas said, slapping Amadeus on the back. He left his hand there and leaned in until his chest rested on Amadeus' shoulder. The look on the nobleman's face nearly caused Lady to burst out laughing as he tried to figure out what was going on and why Nicholas was touching him. Her fellow dragon slayer continued, completely oblivious to the stress he was causing Amadeus by leaning on him. "There's plenty of room at my cousin's home. Unless a rich man like yourself needs two or three rooms to himself?"

"Of course not. I'm sure your accommodations will be more than enough," Amadeus smiled brightly, baring his teeth in a manner that betrayed the pleasant grin. Nicholas patted Amadeus on the shoulder once more before pushing off and heading to his dragon. Amadeus immediately checked his armor for scratches. "I merely find it prudent to have a second option open in case of unforeseen circumstances."

"Such as?" Nicholas asked, pulling himself up onto Martha's back. In the open square, she extended her wings fully, and flapped hard twice.

She shook herself out after a stretch, and Nicholas dropped his helmet over his head. "I am curious what goes on in that head of yours."

"More than you'd understand," Amadeus scoffed. He pulled open his carriage door and pulled himself up, still scowling like a child who'd been denied dessert after dinner. "I suppose we should be off then, since I've already cost us an hour of traveling time."

Lady waved to Nicholas as he and Martha took off, a shining red beacon in the sky. Beasts though they were, even Lady had to admit that at times they had a beauty to them. She watched them disappear over the horizon and hopped into the plush carriage herself. There was more than one sort of beast to deal with in the world, and at the moment, Lady's was a man. Instead of sitting across from him, Lady plopped down in the vacant seat to Amadeus' right.

Amadeus huffed and thumped his fist against the upper wooden wall of the carriage. The carriage sprung to life a second later, and began its journey along the road to follow the dragon. Amadeus opened the bag of croissants and helped himself to one with an uncharacteristic bite. He tore the bread off, and chewed it almost like a petulant brat.

"You don't like Nicholas much," Lady asked, "Do you?"

"I can't say I find his company all that appealing, no," Amadeus said. He became aware of himself it seemed, and pulled down the croissant to his lap. His next nibble was a properly torn piece from the main. "But whether or not I care for his company hardly matters, does it? I am neither a dragon slayer, nor his chosen companion for the hunt."

"But you are my traveling companion," Lady said, reaching over and grabbing the rest of his croissant. She finished it off for him in a single bite. "Or so you claimed. So your opinion matters a little bit."

"Just a little?"

"Look at it this way," Lady said, leaning back into the carriage seat. "It'll be good practice for our Lake Dragon."

"That's what you say about all your dragon kills, isn't it?" Amadeus said, smiling. Just a single hint of amusement.

"It is," Lady said, elbowing Amadeus in the side, "and it's always true."

Chapter 7

THE OLD WITCH received the young rose with open hands. She listened to his plight, his words in her head were airy, the little rose out of breath from the windy flight. His stem ached and he could feel his body slowly draining of life, but he held on enough to ask the Witch to deliver to them a human.

One that would love and adore them.

The old Witch accepted the payment, and set the young rose into a crystal vase full of sparkling water to extend his life for just a few more days. She went to her cabinets and mixed her powders, with both the bird and the young rose watching.

After many hours, she handed the bird a small packet and a list of instructions. The Witch played with her new rose's petals, cackling as the bird flew off from the window.

Just south of the largest river on their continent, was home to the most industrious city on the continent, aptly named South River. Its namesake stretched over ten miles across at the river's widest point, and ran for ninety miles in such a curved way that it wrapped around the city named after it like a comforting snake. Unlike most of the more rural or lightly developed areas that covered most of their homeland, South River was full of tall buildings and smoke covered skies that was more reminiscent of the larger cities from across the oceans. The South River factories dealt mostly in metalworking, transforming ores of all types from iron to gold down into bars for shipment.

The high amounts of precious metal that came in and out during shipments and production, made it a popular target for dragon raids.

"They used to deal with pitiful creatures attacking in and out all the time," Nicholas said, rolling his shoulders. He cracked his neck back and forth, stretching and loosening up from his long dragon ride. Nicholas waved a finger in the air as he continued his story. "Way back when, they practically had a standing army at all times just to fend the beasties off."

Nicholas continued talking about South River history as he helped Drake unpack Amadeus and Lady's belongings from the carriage trunk. They had landed, or driven up in Lady and Amadeus' case, in the back yard of his cousin's home on the outskirts of town. Lucky enough to afford a full sized house on the outer rim of the main city, instead of an apartment in the center downtown, Nicholas' cousin did indeed have enough room for all four guests as their dragon rider friend had claimed.

There was even a small yard just large enough for Martha to lounge in the back. Lady tugged a pack out of the back of the carriage as she watched the dragon sleep, unable to sit still and let Drake handle everything the way Amadeus was keen to. Tethered hard to the ground with a thick chained leash, Martha didn't look like she'd be going anywhere on her own. Nicholas had set up his makeshift tarp over her to keep prying neighbors from getting too curious, and Martha seemed content to nap and be ignored while the rest of them settled in.

Lady had a feeling the tarp wasn't going to fool any of the neighbors that saw the two of them land in the backyard to begin with, but she imagined it would keep them from staring.

Nicholas unlocked the bright red front door with an old brass key sent to him by letter. He picked up a bundle of their supplies, and licked his lip as he pushed open the door with his shoulder. "But the big beastie that we're after, claimed the territory give or take ten years ago. They were doing quite well with only one attack a month from him, if you can imagine."

"I take it that's why they never bothered to contact you before?" Lady asked, taking her own bag into the house. According to Nicholas, his cousin wouldn't be home until dinner time, needing to settle matters in town. As such, the house was vacant and they were told to settle in wherever they liked. House seemed big enough for that to be true. Lady helped herself to the first guest room she found. "Makes sense."

"It does, doesn't it? Let the bigger dragon scare off all the tiny ones. " Nicholas said. He pushed open a second door down the hallway, and allowed Amadeus to walk past him into the room without a care.

Nicholas pushed back his hair and shook his head with a laugh as he turned around and went across the hall to the fourth room after seeing the third claimed by Drake and Amadeus' jewelry crates. "I think they would have let it continue that way forever if the creature's behavior didn't change."

"A good idea in theory, but that seems to be the way it goes," Lady said. She walked out of the room, trying to forget the sight of laced doilies on every surface. Lady reminded herself to be careful to keep her armor from getting snagged on anything from the table clothes to the bed linens. She stretched her arms over her head, and let them drop at her side with a sigh. "Even the big one would need to be taken care of eventually. Even if it's better, an attack a month is still not something you should want to live with."

"Rightly so," Nicholas said. He shut the door to his room, and motioned at the group with a short wave of his hand. "Care to see the town? We've got some time before dinner and we get all the information we need. Might as well look around and get a feel for the city while we're here, am I right?"

"I wouldn't be opposed to a little sight seeing while we're here," Amadeus said, adjusting his traveling cloak over his shining armor. He nodded politely at Nicholas as he adjusted the clasp at the top. "Can't hurt to—"

"Hit two birds with one stone?" Lady finished for him. She grinned and elbowed him in the side enjoying the twitch in his eye as she clinked her dented armor against his polished finish. "I've caught onto your tourist ways. You're a sucker for tourist traps and local delicacies. Just can't help yourself, can you?"

"I really can't," Amadeus said, polishing the spot with his cape. "I won't deny a guilty pleasure when it's been spotted."

Lady caught the smile he tried to hide and sent it back at him with one of her own. Even Drake rolled his eyes from his place on the side wall, his mouth struggling to fight the amusement from showing on his face.

"Tourist traps it is!" Nicholas exclaimed, throwing his arms around the both of Lady and Amadeus' shoulders. He leaned on them from in between and dragged them both toward the front door. "There is plenty to see, so let's get going!"

If Amadeus was ice and calm, Nicholas was all fire and excitement. The boisterous attitude he displayed when he first landed in Honey Farms multiplied ten fold once he'd been in your company for an extended period of time. Nicholas was also rather touchy-feeling, Lady had noticed. He was a man of constant contact: Hugs, shoulder pats, knocked knees, or any other form of touch and clank of armor against armor he could get, he would get. Lady was positive Amadeus would strangle him before the day was out if Nicholas hugged him one more time.

"We still have a couple of hours before dinner," Nicholas said, checking the city square clock. He rubbed his hands together and glanced between his two companions with such joy, that Lady wondered if his energetic disposition was merely some form of overcompensation. Honestly, despite his friendly and outgoing nature, under it all Nicholas gave Lady the vibe that he was rather starved for company. He asked, "Would you care for some afternoon shopping, or a snack? I know a great place around here that has the best candied apples."

"What sort of shops?" Amadeus asked. He fixed his gloves on his hands, stretching out his long fingers under the black fabric. "I don't think I would mind going shopping, if it meant a chance to visit the local import and export depots while I'm here."

"Or we could do something fun instead of business," Lady said. She tapped the edge of her lip and looked around. "Why don't we get one of those candied apples and then do some window shopping?"

"If you insist," Amadeus said. He mock bowed, leaning over with his hand to his chest and his other arm out in recognition toward Lady. Amadeus rose, straightening his cape back out. "Can hardly deny the lady what she wants, now can I?"

"I think that was a pun," Nicholas said, smiling a little as he skipped ahead a few paces. He weaved in and out of the crowded street with ease as he navigated, and Lady didn't need to see his face to know that Nicholas was grinning. "Wasn't it?"

"A gentleman never tells," Amadeus said, rather pleased with himself.

"It was a pun," Lady said, leaning over and tugging on Amadeus' perfectly pressed little cape. "And that means a certain someone who thinks he's funny will be paying for those candied apples."

"Small price to pay," Amadeus said.

And it was true. Lady popped a slice of sweet apple drenched in a red candied coating into her mouth. Amadeus paid for enough candied treats for them to take a couple bags back to to the house house for after dinner and then some. Lady smacked her lips at him when he put away his still very full change purse. *Show off.*

Lady nipped a second slice, and tilted her head to the side. "Hey, Nicholas."

"Yes?" Nicholas replied, pulling his fingers through his hair. His small bag of apples was tied to his belt, already half empty. His appetite matched her own, and that was a scary thought in and of itself. Nicholas stretched with a yawn. "What is it?"

"What's your cousin's name, anyway?" Lady asked, popping another apple into her mouth. She moved to the side to avoid a pushy tourist, lightly brushing against Amadeus' arm. He didn't move away from her, and Lady had to remind herself to stop leaning on him. She cleared her throat and straightened up to break the contact quickly. She shoved another apple piece in her mouth and kept talking while she chewed to the side. "I don't think you ever actually told us."

"Did I not?" Nicholas asked, looking over his shoulder. He laughed and tapped two fingers against his head of curly brown hair. "I suppose it slipped my mind! How silly."

"Yes, there's a word for it," Amadeus muttered under his breath. "Though I can think of a few better ones."

Lady bit her lip to stop the chuckle.

"His name is Everett," Nicholas said. "He works at the City Hall for the Security Council. He mentioned he had a cousin the the slaying business on the offhand, and they drew up the paperwork the next day with official job papers."

"All seems rather formal," Lady said. She dug around in her bag for another slice of candy, and huffed seeing it empty. Amadeus handed her his full bag, and she took it gladly. "He couldn't just write himself?"

"I suppose he could have, but if there's a chance of a large battle near the city, it's probably best if they know about it," Nicholas said. He turned around to face Lady, and began to walk backwards, still somehow managing to avoid the people on the street. "Don't you agree?"

"If you want to be neat and tidy about it," Lady said. She popped another apple in her mouth, and chewed. They really were amazingly delicious. Lady might have to buy more on her way back at this rate. "But still, where's the fun in that?"

"Amadeus?" Nicholas asked, looking around Lady and directly at her companion. His brows drew together, and concern fell on his face. "Is something the matter?"

Lady glanced to the side where Amadeus should have been, and a shop wall stared back at her. She turned around, and spotted Amadeus a few steps back. Lady squeezed the apple slice in her hand, and joined Nicholas in concerned staring. Amadeus had paused on the sidewalk, staring thoughtfully across the street. He squinted, the odd look contorting his face as if he were trying to remember something important.

Perhaps he had forgotten to tell Drake something before they left him alone at Nicholas' house? Lady took a few steps toward him and shook her head. No, he was definitely looking at something or someone with a lot of focus.

All at once, Amadeus' expression lit up into a professional smile, stopping Lady in her tracks. His teeth shone brightly, and he threw his arms out waving his traveling cloak open like a flashy cape. Amadeus dashed across the street and shouted, "Simon! You old dog, how good to see you!"

A slim man a few inches shorter than Amadeus turned at the call, and said "You!" just as Amadeus dropped both of his hands on the stranger's shoulders and drew the man into a tight hug.

Dinner turned from a short briefing from Everett about the dragon they would be facing, into a surprise get together with one of Amadeus' old friends. Lady sat at the head end of the crowded dinner table, with Everett and Nicholas on one side, and Amadeus and Simon on the other. Even with Drake opting to stand near the door (something about servants never eating with their masters), the room was rather crowded. The house had five guest rooms in addition to the master suite, but its dining room was about the size as you'd expect in a house for one.

As such, everyone had a good view of everyone else, with just enough room to sit next to each other without touching. The few inches they had between them was rather welcome, even if she would have preferred more space. But on the other hand, it did give Lady a wonderful chance to see everyone up close and personal.

Nicholas' cousin Everett was similar in appearance: brown hair, tan skin and dark eyes. Everett however, held himself in a manner more fitting of the reserved and calm people of the world, benefitting the paper-pushing profession that Nicholas had shared for him earlier. Rounded glasses sat on Everett's nose, and he preferred to stay quiet while the other four chatted.

Which led back to the surprise guest of the evening: Amadeus' friend Simon.

Simon was a rather timid man, shying away at all the attention he received the second Amadeus hugged him on the street. He dressed well in a nice pair of slacks and button shirt, and his blond hair was styled to be parted on the side. His most distinguishing feature was a rather large rectangular cut emerald he wore on a thick chain around his neck. The gemstone captured all the light in the room, polished bright and perfect. Lady casually touched the spot on her armor that covered her own smaller, more decorative emerald necklace. *Mine is better*, Lady huffed to herself even as Amadeus smiled more at dinner than he had since Lady had met him. He had no troubles patting Simon on the shoulder, or greeting him warmly.

Lady wouldn't lie and say she wasn't absurdly jealous at the familiarity they shared. This was completely different from his play teasing with Agatha, or even how he acted around Lady in his friendliest moments. With Simon, Amadeus had reached a new sincere level of affection, and Lady wondered where the man had been hiding it. Somehow she hadn't considered that Amadeus may have friends of his own.

"Simon works just to the west of here. He specializes in fine gemstones as well, and we do business on occasion," Amadeus had said on the busy street, with his arm around Simon's shoulder. He had started into introductions the second everyone caught up with him. "It hadn't even occurred to me that I might see my old friend on this trip, and yet here he is!"

"N-nice to meet you," Simon had stuttered out, eyes darting around. He curled in on himself, as if the glances of Lady and Nicholas were spotlights centered on him. "It's a surprise for me, too."

Nicholas had spared no time inviting him to dinner, and Amadeus insisted that the man accept when Simon initially declined. Lady thought him mousey, truth be told. Simon had his own charm though in a way, even under all that shyness. His eyes were sharp and a beautiful brown that was almost too rich and sharp for his timid nature.

"I'm so glad I ran into you, Simon," Amadeus said, cutting into the steak on his plate. He sliced off a square and popped it in his mouth, almost too cheery. "It's been so long since we've seen each other."

Simon fiddled with the emerald on his necklace, twisting it in his fingers back and forth. As he rolled it over, Lady could see his name carved into the back in a fine script. It was engraved deep, and the letters covered the entire top half of the emerald cut gem. Simon dropped the necklace and the large pendant bounced on his chest. "Same, same. You're just as I remembered you, only with less rings."

"Rings?" Lady asked, working on her second steak.

"He used to have a thing for them," Simon muttered. He lifted his fork, twirling it in the air as he spoke. "Big old ruby rings. Had a ton of them."

Lady glanced at Amadeus' empty fingers. "Wore them over your gloves, did you?"

"Once in a while," Amadeus said. He held his knife up and waved it back and forth in the air. "I don't think it's a crime to alter my tastes now and again to shake things up."

"If you say so," Simon said. His plate was barely touched, and he shoved around the peas on the side into the mashed potatoes with his fork. "What are you doing here again?"

"I'm accompanying the lovely Lady here to the Ruby Mines," Amadeus said. He sliced another piece of steak in a quick slide of the knife. He bit the steak off his fork and grinned at Simon. "We ended up taking an unexpected pit stop here for her and the gentlemen Nicholas to take care of the dragon problem this city seems to have."

"Dragon problem?" Simon asked, swallowing. He took a bite of his mashed potato and pea mixture. "What problem would that be? I've been here for a few days and no one's said anything."

"He has been absent his usual rounds for a few months," Nicholas said. He scraped the last of his potatoes off his dish as Everett ate quietly beside him. Nicholas made sure to finish chewing his next mouthful before continuing his story. "So most people think he's fled the coop, while we think he's just saving up for a big strike."

"Interesting theory, isn't it?" Amadeus asked, patting Simon on the shoulder.

"Yeah, that's one way to put it," Simon said. He pulled his plate over and started to eat with more earnest, devouring everything on the plate from the steak to the vegetables. He licked the side of his mouth and shrugged. "Good luck with that."

Lady pulled out the bag of candied apples and popped one in her mouth. As the others continued to chat about their upcoming dragon fight, she couldn't help but notice that Amadeus' thigh was pressed hard up against Simon's.

Chapter 8

THE BIRD DELIVERED the instructions back to the valley and its ruby roses, the original messenger fated to live out the last of his days in a vase on the counter.

The ingredient list was short, but the items rare.

The roses gathered together in council to decide on how they could acquire each item on the list, and what more sacrifices might have to be made in order to get them back to the valley.

They had long decided there was truly no price too high for this. The first sacrifice was one of many, and many more would come. But the roses knew it would be worth it.

It was almost within their grasp.

It was around ten o'clock when Lady and Nicholas left with Everett to start their investigation and hunt of the South River dragon. They had their privacy for the information, as Amadeus and Simon had left earlier that morning to discuss business with local gem dealers that worked with the city's precious metal imports and exports. Amadeus said they'd be back after a late lunch, since he wanted to catch up on some more personal matters in person with Simon while he had the chance. Letters were tedious, and Amadeus had been neglectful with them anyway.

"Why waste the opportunity?" he had said.

Lady had smiled as she waved to them both, but the frown came soon after. She did her best to disguise it with a neutral purse of the lips, but Nicholas must have noticed the mood shift, because he taunted Lady with the leftover apple treats soon after they left.

"If you keep frowning like that, I'm going to give these to Martha," Nicholas had said, tossing the small bag of treats up and down in his palm. "I bet she'd like them."

Lady was more than happy to steal the entire bag from him, and munched down heartily while he made playful grabs around her as he tried to retrieve the stolen bag. When the moment of fun ended, the two of them waved goodbye to Drake and Martha, and were on their way to the center of the city.

Everett brought Lady and Nicholas to City Hall, and they were finally able to discuss the plans that were delayed thanks to the unexpected company during last night's dinner. Lady tilted her head all the way back to see the decorations that were carved into the stone blocks far above on the towering entrance archway. The hall itself was busy and packed with people running in and out, back and forth, and all with their arms full of papers and folders. Both Lady and Nicholas sighed in relief when Everett closed the door on his small, but relatively empty office.

There was one other in the room when they arrived who was introduced as Everett's co-worker. Her name was Brianna of the South River, Third Family. Lady thought the woman was rather pretty, with glasses on her face and bouncing curls on her head. She had been one of the first who agreed upon Everett's plan to find out just what their large dragon was up to, and took no time in starting the brief the second the door had been shut.

"We think that his cave is somewhere in this region," Brianna said, pointing at a spot on the map on the other side of the river. She pushed her glasses higher on her nose, and crossed her arms in exaggerated frustration. "But we're not sure."

"No one's seen it?" Lady asked. Large Dragons' hoards and homes were usually well known to the villages and towns that lived closest to them. It was hard to miss something that giant flying in and out and not know where they were going. Unless they lived in the mountains and took refuge behind the giant protrude rocks and caves, but that was another issue entirely. "That's hard to believe."

"He flies too far away to follow," Everett added, drawing a circle on the map around South River with his finger. "We're a long-distance raid trip for him, so it makes sense we've never seen his home."

"And no other towns have seen your dragon menace?" Nicholas asked, rubbing his chin. "If he's commuting, surely he claims home elsewhere?"

"I don't think he eats where he lives, so to speak," Brianna said, twisting a pen cap between her fingers. "Or that's the thought."

"Only one way to find out," Lady said. She slapped her sword on her side. "Point us in the direction that he goes and we'll follow it, hunt him down, and slay him."

"I doubt it'll be that easy," Brianna said, scoffing and throwing her pen on the table.

"It's exactly that easy," Nicholas said, studying the map on the wall. He leaned in close until his nose was a few inches from the surface, grinning and running his eyes across every town name and hill. "That's our job."

Everett rubbed the side of his head with the tips of his fingers and sucked in a breath. He tapped the map. "You have to have a better plan than that. Who knows how long that'll take you?"

"As long as it takes," Nicholas said. He saluted from the top of his head and winked. "But don't worry, with my Martha and Miss Lady here, I have a feeling we'll take care of it before you know it."

Brianna and Everett watched Nicholas and Lady with the same disbelieving stare that always did wonders for motivating those without plans to win via spite.

And Lady was all for that.

"I think that my cousin was going to hit me," Nicholas said, laughing as he stepped into the busy street. He stretched his arms high over his head and snapped his fingers in the air. Nicholas dropped them at his side and stretched them back behind him, locking his fingers together and twisting his spine. Lady heard his spine crack. "After the third time we told them our plan, I'm fairly certain he wanted to."

"If he didn't hit you, Brianna was most certainly going to deck me," Lady said. She scrunched her nose in a grin, stretching the skin on the side of her face. Lady scratched where the smooth scarred flesh met the rest. "Is it really so hard to understand that we track dragons for a living? Who needs a detailed plan?"

"Bureaucrats," Nicholas said, with a deadpanned expression that lasted for all of three seconds before his grin broke out again. Nicholas dropped a couple coins into a street vendor's hand, and bought a few regular apples. He tossed one at Lady, and took a bite of his own. "What more do you need to know?"

"When lunch is." Lady looked up at the town clock, holding her hand over her eyes. She took a large bite out the apple, and wiped the slight drip of juice off the side of her lip. "Because this snack is hardly going to tide me over."

"I agree one hundred percent," Nicholas said. He took another bite of his apple and tilted his head at the people walking by. "I wonder if your moody friend and his mysterious buddy have finished up yet. They could join us."

"Amadeus isn't moody," Lady said, pouting as she ate the last mouthful off the fruit. She tossed her apple core in a bin as they passed. "He's just quiet and keeps to himself."

"Moody and brooding," Nicholas said, grinning over his shoulder. Laughter danced in his eyes, and Lady nearly hit him. She restrained herself, which was for the best. Nicholas saved himself as he continued, "But I suppose I'm seeing him on a bad day, yes? He didn't exactly want to come on this side trip, did he?"

"Yes," Lady said. She rubbed the back of her neck and sighed. "It would be nice to meet up with them for lunch though. It's late enough, isn't it?"

Nicholas nodded, "More or less. We did spend quite some time convincing Everett and Brianna we knew what we were doing."

"You remember where they said they were going to be?" Lady asked.

"Town square, I believe," Nicholas said, taking another bite out of his apple. He pointed down the street toward the bend that led to the main street. "Under the clock, yes?"

Lady followed Nicholas toward the town square through the straight streets. The people milled about going about their daily lives around them in the hustle and bustle city life claimed to fame. Lady breathed in the air, and smiled when she spotted Amadeus under the town clock. She smiled brighter when she noticed that he was alone.

"Where'd your friend Simon go?" Lady asked, stepping up. She put her hand over her eyes and faked glancing around. "Thought he was hanging around for afterwards?"

"Simon got caught up in a lovely conversation with a merchant who primarily deals in emeralds," Amadeus said, turning. He pointed at his chest and tapped there for a few seconds. "If you noticed that rather large pendent of his, I'm sure you can take a guess what happened after that."

"Oh, poor little ruby dealer," Lady said, slapping him on the back of the shoulder. "You got dumped for a prettier gem."

"I don't think I'd go that far," Amadeus said. He sniffed and held his nose in the air. He licked the side of his lips, and then tapped Lady's armor right over the collarbone. "But it can't be too bad of a gem if you're so fond of it, too."

Amadeus smiled and took his hand back. He ruined the compliment as he tagged on, "But rubies are far better."

Lady managed half of a "Hey!" objection when Nicholas chimed in, "For once we agree, my friend! Rubies are the far superior gem."

"You're only saying that because your dragon is covered in them," Lady said, rolling her eyes. She knocked both of them in the arm at once. "And he makes a living off them. I think you both might be biased."

"You speak truth, and I do not disagree," Nicholas said. He rubbed his hands together, and linked arms with both Lady and Amadeus on each of his sides without a second thought. "So our trio is together again! Let us get lunch."

Amadeus rolled his eyes as Nicholas dragged them down the street in tow, and Lady couldn't help but giggle.

This wasn't so bad.

Lady knocked on Amadeus' door, a quick wrap with the back of her knuckles. She rolled up her sleeves, and tapped her foot on the ground. The lacy doilies on the hallway bench mocked her as she waited. What was it with Everett and his obsession with lacy white things everywhere? The door opened a few seconds later, and Amadeus slicked his hair down. His night shirt hung open just enough, and Lady bit her lip at the pleasant view.

"Need something, or just looking for company?" Amadeus asked. He buttoned the top of his shirt with one hand, and stepped back to let Lady in. "It is rather late, you know."

"First, I suppose I'm curious how you got the one room in the house free of doilies," Lady said putting her hands on her hips. She pouted lifting the edge of a perfectly normal flower-embroidered runner that was atop the dresser. Lovely dark colors of red and deep green. "Not a speck of it in here anywhere."

"Just lucky I suppose," Amadeus said. He closed the door behind them both. "Though I'm sure you're not here to comment on my guest room. What's the trouble?"

"We're planning on leaving early in the morning, so I wanted to get things straight before we headed off," Lady said, tugging on the end of her braid. She pulled over a chair and spun it around to straddle the seat. Amadeus sat on the edge of his bed, crossing one leg over the other and leaning on his knees. Lady folded her arms over the chair back and waved a hand. "You know, find out where you're headed after we leave tomorrow, and figure out where a good place to meet up might be."

Amadeus rubbed the tips of his fingers together, the milky white skin smooth and soft. He nodded slowly, eyebrow raised. "I see."

"Unless you wanted to travel alone back to Ruby Mines, of course," Lady blurted out rather quickly. She cleared her throat and grabbed her braid. "That'd be understandable. I mean, we only just met and there's no reason we have to travel together."

"My original plan was to tag along, actually," Amadeus said, setting his chin on the back of his knuckles. His elbow rested on the top of his knee, and he leaned against his arm like he longed for a plush chair to lounge in. Amadeus shrugged in that way that only rich people could seem to manage, that gave him the appearance of a man without a care in the world. "We're both going to the same place, and I've found company is a rather pleasant way to travel. Since I'm in no hurry to get home, I might as well wait for you don't you think?"

"I think you summarized that quite nicely," Lady said. She pressed her knuckles into the side of her cheek, and licked the back of her teeth. The room was quiet, and the air was almost too stuffy for the way her heart was beating a thousand miles a minute. Lady concentrated on the click of the clock in the corner of the room and tried not to think on how they were alone together. "And your company has been rather pleasant, too. For as little as we've had."

"Always time for more," Amadeus said. He got up and began to pull back the sheets and blankets on his bed. Lady's heart skipped a beat. Amadeus turned and waved his hand at Lady, motioning her toward the door. "And right now, it's time for sleep. We have an early morning, don't we?"

"Well, Nicholas and I do," Lady said, saying the words slowly as the crushing disappointment that an invitation was not following the bed sheets being folded back. Lady rubbed the base of her jaw with her forefingers. "I don't think you have to wake up all that early if you're just going to be waiting here for us."

"I told you I'm going to tag along, and I see no reason why I wouldn't for this little detour as well," Amadeus said, looking over his shoulder. He gently shifted his armor on the floor just a few more inches in line with the rest. "That means for the dragon slaying part as well."

"It'll be dangerous, you know," Lady said. She smacked the top of the chair back with her palm while glaring at Amadeus' back. "We've talked about this, briefly, but we have talked about it."

"And as I have mentioned before, I can more than take care of myself," Amadeus replied. He tapped the top of his head with his finger, smirking so coyly Lady felt she was being mocked. Amadeus rested his hip on the side table next to the bed. "It's not all brawn out there, and someone has to keep an eye on you."

Lady squeezed the back of the chair. "I won't be alone."

"Yes, I remember Nicholas and his dragon," Amadeus said. He folded his blanket edge into a perfect triangle and sat on the clean sheets underneath. Amadeus pushed the blanket corner farther back, before leaning down prop his boots up straight against the side table. Lady found herself glancing at his pale, bare feet and the lack of callouses renewed her determination to keep him home. Amadeus ignored her inner thoughts, continuing on as he said, "As lovely as they both are, I'd prefer to tag along than sit and wait at home twiddling my thumbs."

"And I'd prefer if I didn't have to worry about you," Lady said, standing. She pointed at his armor on the floor, set out neatly and organized. Even the cape was folded into a tight square, resting on top of the breastplate. "You said it yourself that armor down there was just for show. Which means you will be a liability, so the argument is the same as before with that Lake Dragon we'll be after soon. You're not going."

"I'll see you in the morning, and I am going to come along. Whether you want me to or not," Amadeus said, something hard sneaking into his voice that left no room for argument. He spun his finger in a circle as he slipped his feet under the blankets. He pat down the blanket above his legs, crossing his arms over it. Amadeus said, almost condescendingly, "It's late. Do get some rest, as I plan to get mine while I can so we'll both be ready tomorrow."

Lady turned the chair and placed it back against the wall. "Then I guess I'll see you in the morning."

"Sweet dreams," Amadeus said.

Lady slammed the door behind her, breathing heavily for a few moments. He wasn't going to change his mind. Amadeus was going to fight his way on this trip no matter what Lady said. She growled, and bit the side of her thumb. *Stubborn, stupid man.*

That wasn't going to do at all.

Nicholas yelped like a dog whose tail had been stepped on when Lady dumped his armor on his bare belly. He sat up shoving the armor off like it was a spider that had fallen on his face, and grabbed his blanket to cover his equally bare lower half. Nicholas blinked a few times, before his vision focused and he turned his head toward her. "Lady? What are you doing?"

"We're leaving now," she hissed. She threw another piece of armor at him, followed by his leathers and undershirts. "So get up and get dressed. Not in an hour, not in a few minutes. Right now."

Nicholas turned and looked at the clock on his dresser while clutching his mixed bundle of clothes and metal shielding. "It's near one in the morning. Why so early?"

"Because Amadeus is a spoiled little rich boy who doesn't know how to take 'no' for an answer," Lady answered. She shoved Nicholas' helmet at him and into his hands. He dropped the rest of his armor in a clatter when he was unable to hold both. "And we're leaving before he can follow along and get himself killed."

"Ah, I suppose that's good moti—"

"Now. Move it," Lady said, cutting him off. She opened the door and pointed her finger straight at his face. "We're leaving in twenty minutes."

"Yes, Ma'am," Nicholas said. He nodded twice, clutching his helmet to his chest like a child's teddy. Nicholas grinned nervously, shrinking down in his bed as she glared. "Twenty minutes."

Lady shut the door to let the naked man dress, and sucked in a breath. She went to stand before Amadeus' room and leaned her ear against the wall to make sure that he was still asleep after all that racket. She could hear his soft breathing through the door, and held her hand to her chest. Lady touched the necklace there and nodded to herself.

Lady was dressed and ready to go within the specified twenty minutes she had dictated to Nicholas. He was outside and waiting with Martha before Lady had finished getting ready herself. At least one of these two men knew how to listen to reason. Lady listened to him whisper apologies to Martha for their late night departure and waking her, while she wrote a short note to let Everett and Amadeus know where they had run off to in the middle of the night. Lady pulled her hair up and away from her face, tightening her braid into a tight bun on the back of her head. A few loose strands fell down, and she blew them out of the way.

She shoved a second, much shorter note under Amadeus' door, and left to join Nicholas without another word. The note was short and simple:

Sorry, but not worth the risk. See you when we get back.
-Lady

Chapter 9

IT TOOK EIGHT weeks for the ruby roses to complete the witch's spell. The work had been difficult and tragic, so much so that they refused to record the events that had transpired for future generations. The lives lost in the spell's production were uncountable, and would go down in their history as the worst tragedy they had ever sustained.

But they pressed on.

It had to be worth it.

On the fourth day of the eight week since they began, a small green sprout began to grow in the center of their field.

"I do believe Amadeus will be quite cross with us when he awakes," Nicholas yelled over his shoulder. Between the wind and the metal of his helmet it was near impossible to hear him. Lady kept her gaze forward, concentrating on what he said in case something important came up. Despite being a hundred or so feet in the air on the back of a dragon, Nicholas weathered it all like he were out for a pleasant horse ride on a dirt road. Casual and relaxed, Nicholas asked, "Don't you think?"

"He'll deal with it," Lady muttered back through the thick scarf covering her mouth. She clutched hard to Nicholas' waist as they soared in the air, angry to admit she was rather nervous about this whole dragon riding affair. The flap of Martha's wings were heavy beside them, the gemstone scales scraping against each other in a soft, screeching sound. It reminded Lady of another dragon's shrieking scales, but it was still a welcome distraction with the ground very, very far down below. Lady locked her eyes onto a spot on Nicholas' armor. "How'd you talk me into this!"

"Flying is the only way to travel!" Nicholas laughed. He wrapped Martha's reins around his palms twice and kept them taught and the dragon's head straight. "Once you've flown dragon, you can never return to little horse drawn carriages."

"Walking would be preferable to this!" Lady shouted. She rocked in the seat along with the slight slide of Martha's back as it moved up and down. "Walking! Do you hear me?"

"Keep talking like that and you'll insult Martha," Nicholas said. He looked down past her neck at the ground and hummed. "Her hearing is quite good, I'll have you know. Just keep your eyes out for a large dragon flying about, would you?"

"Martha can be insulted." Lady shifted her leg, scooting it up along the saddle. The blanket underneath shifted against the dragon's scales, scrunching up as the ruby plates slid against each other. She kicked Martha's side lightly, letting loose a few ruby scales to fall down to the earth below. "Stupid flying dragons."

"Yes, yes. It takes some getting used to," Nicholas said. He tugged on Martha's rein to the left and the dragon turned in that direction obediently. She let out a small puff of fire aimed downward, and glided along calmly. "But this really is the best way to travel."

Lady smacked her face into Nicholas' back before she looked down past the wings. The world below them sped by like blurred lines. "How can you see anything down there moving this fast?"

"You get used to it," Nicholas said. He placed both reins into one hand and reached down to pet Martha's neck. He patted the scales roughly, and laughed. "And Martha is looking, too, I'll have you know. If her hearing is great, Martha's vision is even better. Her eyes are fantastic for this."

"You're quite fond of her, aren't you?" Lady asked, twisting her fingers into the leather belt at Nicholas' waist.

"Against my better judgement, I rather am," Nicholas said. He rolled his shoulders back, bumping into Lady's face. Nicholas corrected by scooting forward in his saddle a few inches. "Sorry about that. Not used to having a guest rider, you know."

"Martha's a one-rider dragon?"

"She's easily big enough to fit two, but not many other people are willing to share," Nicholas hummed. He pat Martha's lower horns, and she could hear his sigh through the helmet. "There are other dragon riders back home, of course, but Martha's so much bigger than their steeds they don't trust her."

"She is a rather big girl for a Mini," Lady said. She loosened her death grip on Nicholas' waist, relaxing in the saddle. She breathed in and out slowly. If Nicholas could be so calm, so could she! Lady said, "A few more feet and she'd almost qualify for a Medium Dragon. Takes a lot of talent to tame a beast that size."

"Just a loving touch," Nicholas said, ending with a little hum. Lady leaned back in the saddle and looked up at the white puffs all around them. He was calmer up here in the air. His energy and enthusiasm brought to a still quiet as they soared above everything in the clouds. Nicholas continued his gentle petting of Martha's side. "That's all there is to it."

"A loving touch, huh?" Lady asked, resting her face on his back. "I wonder if that's even possible for a dragon."

"You'll never know until you try, hm?" Nicholas said. He turned his head back and hummed lightly. "Most dragons are monsters, but I've found they're a bit more varied than we think."

Nicholas patted Martha's side as he spoke, indicating his own bias fairly well. Lady licked her lips under the scarf and watched down below. "I think I'll stay focused on the ones that are monsters for now, if you don't mind."

"Fair enough," Nicholas admitted. Martha's glide jerked downward, and her speed picked up. Nicholas straightened his back with a jerk, and pointed below, leaning close to Martha's neck. Lady looked down his arm and grinned wide. She slapped his side lightly with her hand as he said, "Our lucky day! We won't need to find the nest at all."

"No we won't," Lady agreed, glancing over Martha's side. Even from this height, their target was unmistakable below. "Look what we found."

The dragon was large, easily four to five times the size of Martha, and covered from its snout to the end of its tail in rough sandstone scales. Martha flew lower to get a better look, and Lady took note of any other important features outside of the scale type. The dragon's head was long, and had four long wavy whiskers coming off the sides of its cheeks. The rest of the beast was much wider past the thick neck, and Lady confirmed the dragon was heavily armored with the gritty brown scale plates. The dragon flew low and slow to the ground, almost crawling compared to Martha's glide. There was no mistaking it, from the description they'd received, this was the dragon that they'd been hired to hunt down.

"It's going to be tough getting through those scales," Nicholas said, keeping Martha high enough that the dragon who had paused to drink at the riverbed couldn't see them. "Sandstone Dragons are a nasty bunch."

"Sandstone's near impossible to break with a sword," Lady said. She leaned back and reached into the large pack that was strapped onto Martha's back behind the saddle. Lady grinned wide, pulling out a war hammer from the varied selection of lances Nicholas had collected through the years. She patted the thing in her hand, turning it to show off the large flat heat. "But that's why we brought this."

"Yes," Nicholas said. He watched the ground below, his body still and a new air of concentration falling over him like a blanket. He breathed evenly, and Lady was impressed with yet another new side to him. His intense attentiveness seemed to carry the energy of his friendly nature with the calm of his flying. However, it lasted for all of three seconds. Nicholas laughed loudly, breaking out of his moment of seriousness, and turned toward Lady. "Alright then! He's a tank, but he's still a slow, lumbering beastie! You distract on the ground, and Martha and I will try to get on his back. You smack, I stab in the broken bits. Good plan?"

"Fine, but how am I getting to the—"

"Good plan!" Nicholas said. He yanked the reins and Martha dove. Lady yelped, clutching to Nicholas' back and the hammer like they were here only lifelines. Before she had a chance to adjust to the new speed, Nicholas turned and grabbed Lady by the back of her armor. "Ready?"

"Ready for what!" Lady screamed at him.

"The dive!" The moment they were next to the ground, Nicholas gave her a great shove. Lady dropped from the dragon's back and rolled on the ground to stick a landing. She managed to hold onto the hammer, and vowed to whack Nicholas upside the head with it when this was done. Nicholas shouted as Martha climbed back up into the sky, "Good luck!"

"I'll good luck you!" Lady shouted back, swinging the hammer up into her hand. Their target dragon glared down at her, its bright yellow eyes aglow with anger. The fire its mouth was enough to have Lady shout, "Later!"

The beast landed on the ground, swinging its giant paw at her, the claws fully extended and ferocious. She leapt to the side, just missing the claws as they dug a full foot into the ground. The dragon lifted a chunk of earth back out and threw it at her. Lady hit the dirt clump with the hammer, and ran for the side.

Just as they predicted, the dragon was big and heavy which made it slow. They wouldn't have to worry about a flying fight, as the Sandstone Dragon was far more capable fighting on good old land. The dragon's lumbering movements made it easy for Lady to dash around its side before the monster could turn and follow her. She swung her hammer back, and with every inch of strength she could muster, slammed it into a sizable scale on the side of its belly.

The sandstone didn't so much as crack, and but the scale did manage to chip the edge of the hammer.

"Perfect," Lady muttered under her breath. The dragon's head peeked around the side of its gut, and Lady felt the heat. She ran toward its back and ducked under its tail. Lady made it to the other side just as the burst of fire past her back. "Perfect!"

Lady's heart beat in her chest, and her armor clanked loudly in her ears as she ran. Trustworthy armor blessed her profession, and Lady appreciated it all the more again and again as she ducked and weaved under the dragons legs and back. The beast's head and claws followed her, breathing fire and grabbing chunks of rock and dirt as it attempted to grab her.

Run, dodge, smack with the hammer, curse, repeat.

The ever so wonderful pattern of the distraction worked wonders, but Lady could only keep it up for so long. She either needed a cracked scale that she could sneak by to wound it with, or Nicholas needed to hurry his ass up and land on the dragon's back.

She made it fully around the dragon a second time, and swung the hammer back. She aimed for the scale she had hit the first time and slammed the hammer's head hard against the sandstone chunk. This time, it cracked. The stone showed fractures, to Lady's relief, but it hadn't broken yet. Lady jumped at the fire licking her back and cursed herself. *Pay attention!* The Sandstone Dragon had noticed her score and was now on full alert. The beast pushed himself to his limit in speed, grabbing and snapping at Lady with his claws and teeth.

It roared and growled, making a right racket, but Lady was on a roll now.

Instead of making a full circle around the beast, she ducked down and went right under its belly. Dangerous, as the beast could just drop down at any moment, but Lady was feeling the adrenaline pumping in her veins. She slid out from under it, just as the large stomach dropped and hit the ground. She bounced with the weight of the movement, and laughed as the dragon missed her. Lady spotted her cracked scale and ran full sprint at it. She swung the hammer and smacked the crack dead center on the spiderweb fracture.

The scale shattered.

The large chunks of sandstone fell away, and the dragon hissed. Lady turned the hammer in her hand, and slung it over her back. She locked it into a leather strap she'd borrowed from Nicholas, keeping it out of the way, and drew her sword. Lady made another lap around the dragon, same as the first. *Don't get grabbed, don't get burned.* The desperation of the Sandstone dragon increased, and it tripped on its own legs as he tried to turn after her.

The dragon's head hit the ground with a thud, disturbing the earth. Lady took her cue, and ran to the first side where a bit of tan flesh was a glaring white against the brown, dirty scales. Lady charged, ramming the tip of her sword into the newly exposed weak point. The blade dipped into the exposed flesh, slicing straight through.

The dragon screamed.

A horrific high pitched wail filled the area, deafening and absolute in agony despite the relatively small wound. The harder the scales, the more delicate the dragon underneath. Size never mattered much when it came down to this one fact of dragons. Lady shoved her sword in harder, the sizzling red blood pouring down the steel of her blade and onto her gloves and armor. She yanked it back out, and ran back just as a tail whipped around attempting to knock her off her feet. The blood dribbled down the side of the dragon's scales, bubbling as it hit the ground. The heat of it was intense, cooking anything that it touched near instantly.

The Sandstone Dragon turned toward Lady, mouth open wide and fire forming. She smiled at it, and pointed up.

Martha dove into the Sandstone Dragon's head, grabbing it with her claws and scraping at everything she could reach. Her claws did very little against the rough scales, but they dug into the fleshy part of the eye with ease. Martha hissed and screamed alongside the wailing Sandstone dragon, gnawing at his horns and keeping her claws firmly in its eyes.

Nicholas dropped onto the dragons back, and Lady watched on as he managed to keep his balance on the squirming and writhing dragon. Years of riding a dragon must have helped, as Nicholas ran across the dragon's back as easily as if he were crossing a flat field. Lady decided it was no good for those two to have all the fun.

As Martha kept the head busy, and Nicholas searched the back for those loose scales that revealed the weak point on the neck for the killing blow, Lady helped herself to the hammer again. Distracted as it was, she could freely hit the same scales over and over again until they shattered. Lady had removed four scales, by the time she heard Nicholas shout "Got it!"

Martha released the head and flew back and far away as the dragon tumbled over. Nicholas clutched hard at the sword he had driven into the base of the dragon's neck. A thick scale leaned on him as he twisted the sword harder and further down into the base of the neck. Blood poured out over the dragon's back and hit the ground in streams as it came from the delicate artery. Nicholas pushed his sword farther down, so that the handle was near buried in the scalding hot flesh.

The dragon jerked once, the remaining good eye open wide. Lady backed up as the pupil dilated and the dragon collapsed. It breathed heavily twice, before the entire mass of it stilled. Nicholas shivered on it's back, his hands still buried into the dragon with his sword. He pulled them both free, and rested it on the dragon's back in a wheezing lump as he caught his breath again.

Nicholas laughed like a mad man a second later, ripping off his helmet. He dumped it in his lap, and sprawled out on the dragon's back. Martha landed next to him and yawned as she scratched her claws against the sandstone scales. Nicholas patted her on the side from his prone position, whispering something that sounded like "good girl," before leaning over the edge of the dead dragon and yelling, "What rush! Am I right?"

"What took you so long!" Lady yelled back at him. She shook the hammer in the air at him, smiling brightly in contradiction to her angry yelling. "You couldn't have come in sooner?"

Nicholas slid down the side of the dragon, hitting the ground hard.

Bits of the dragon's blood clung to his armor, but his face was still clean. His brown eyes sparkled as he approached Lady. "We were having too much fun watching you! Your reputation did not lie, I am more than happy to admit."

Lady slung the hammer over her shoulder and huffed. His grin was infections, and Lady found herself sharing it without complaint. "Of course you were."

Nicholas winked at her, before taking back his borrowed hammer and heading back to their kill with a happy strut in his step. Lady blew her hair out of her face and took a well deserved seat.

Using a broken scale as her chair, Lady sat a few good feet away from the corpse. Martha rested beside her, yawning every so often, but mostly content to sit and sunbathe like a large cat. Her bridle and reins were in a heap next to her, Nicholas having removed them just before Martha attacked the Sandstone Dragon. It was odd seeing the dragon without them, truth be told, no matter how much it spoke of Nicholas' trust in the beast.

Lady glanced up at the sun, and sighed. The hour was nearing ten o'clock and Lady was more than ready to pack up and leave. "Are you finished yet?"

"Almost got it!" Nicholas said, slamming the hammer hard again into a side scale. The sandstone chipped away with each hit, and the fifth and final scale fell to the ground after two more good whacks. Nicholas wiped his brow, and sit the hammer on the ground. "Finally."

Lady rolled her eyes back as he cut open the dragon's side just under the neck and above the top of the beast's rib cage. The sword sliced cleanly through the unprotected flesh, and just beyond that, Nicholas easily opened the dragon's Hoard Gut. Martha got to her feet in a quick rush, and landed behind Nicholas as the mass of gems and golden things poured out onto the ground.

The man whistled as he sorted through the dragon's traveling stash on his knees in the middle of it. Nicholas pulled out a towel and wiped the sticky mucus off the items as he picked them up. He held up a rather large sapphire, freshly cleaned with the rag. Nicholas threw it over his shoulder and Martha caught it in her mouth. She swallowed, the gem traveling down the neck into Martha's own Hoard Gut hidden behind her ruby scales.

Lady winced as Nicholas continued this odd little habit: Pick out something nice, throw it over his shoulder, and Martha caught it. Every once in a while he'd stand up and wave something particularly large or shiny. Martha's eyes would follow it as if it were the last and most precious thing on earth. Nicholas would throw it hard across the field and she'd leap after it with strong legs and wings to catch it.

It was practically a game.

"That part of the deal of riding a dragon?" Lady asked, as more and more of the precious things disappeared into Martha's stomach. She was oddly reminded of someone playing catch with a dog. "You give it your spoils?"

"Have you ever met a dragon that was happy with an empty hoard?" Nicholas asked, turning his head. He grabbed a handful of golden necklaces, looked them over before shrugging and and stuffed them in a pouch on his side. Lady lifted her eyebrow at him, and he winked. "For later."

"Those aren't ours, you know," Lady said. She rubbed the side of her head, once again wondering why she even bothered to point it out. No one ever listened. Certainly not Amadeus, so why should Nicholas? Not when he had a greedy dragon to appease. "We should return them to their owners."

"My dear, whoever owned these is most likely dead," Nicholas said, repeating a familiar phrase that Lady had heard before. He absently tossed another sapphire to Martha, and she swallowed it down contently. "Might as well not let them go to waste."

Lady did not refute his statement, and instead walked over to the hoard of shiny things. Her own small stash of bait was heavy at her side now, and she had to admit she was tempted. Why continue to pay Agatha for gems to tempt and taunt when she could just continue using the spoils of her own kills. Finished with the game of catch, Martha bypassed Nicholas and began to eat the gems for herself, shoving aside the red rubies that she had in abundance already. Dragons clearly had no care for second-hand goods.

And if their owners were dead…

"Wait!" Lady shouted. Martha's snout had shoved aside a small stack, revealing a glittering stone. She shoved Martha aside, pressing on her head and getting between Nicholas and the dragon. Lady knelt and her hands shook as she picked up the large trinket from the dragon's hoard. She covered her mouth as it sat in her palm. "Oh, no."

She held a large, rectangular emerald pendant on a thick chain.

Chapter 10

THE SMALL BLUE flower was unlike anything they had seen before. Instead of stone for its petals and stems, it was soft and delicate. The petals flexed and moved in the wind, like the feathers of a bird's wing. A lovely flower, warm and beautiful in their cold and chilled world.

It was a different sort of beauty, that made them both adore it and yet also envious of it.

The bud grew to an incomparable size, nearly four to five times the size of the largest ruby rose. However, it would be another three moons before it bloomed and revealed their most coveted prize.

"You will have to tell him," Nicholas said, rubbing the back of his neck. Martha had devoured the rest of the dragon's cache, leaving the ground empty of all but the dragon's blood stains and a pile of useless rubies. Lady clutched the remaining green pendant to her chest and bit her lip. Nicholas put a hand on her shoulder. "You can't hide it, Lady."

"I know, I know," Lady said. She glared down at the offending emerald and her breath shook as she exhaled. "But he was just so happy to see his friend. What do I tell him? Oh! Sorry! Be glad you saw your friend for a day because now he's been eaten!"

"Maybe not quite that coarsely, but yes," Nicholas said. He hugged Lady, holding her tight and rubbing her back armor. Nicholas whispered, "That is exactly what you tell him. In this world, we should always be thankful for every minute we are together, because they might be gone in a flash."

"Because of things like him," Lady said, glaring at the Sandstone dragon. Even dead, it managed to cause harm.

"Sometimes yes," Nicholas said. He released Lady from his bone crushing hug, and rubbed her arm. "At the very least, he will know what has happened. Nothing worse than trying to visit years later and not realizing he's been dead the whole time."

"That's true," Lady said. She bit the side of her thumb, and tried not to think of the joy that had lit up his green eyes when he talked with Simon at dinner. "But it will still hurt him."

"You care for this man very much, don't you?" Nicholas asked, rubbing his hands together. Martha came and nudged his side, her mouth heading for his pack. He shoved her head down, and hissed, "Not now."

"I don't know." Lady shook her head and clutched the emerald pendant in her hand. She swallowed. "We barely know each other and we've only just met, but."

"It is alright," Nicholas said. He tugged lightly on her forearm. "You hardly need to figure it all out right now. All you have to do is breathe and get ready to deliver the bad news to him."

"Yes," Lady answered. She counted to ten, breathing slowly in and out. Lady did that a second time, before shoving the necklace into her pouch. She kicked a sandstone scale for good measure before dragging her feet over to Martha. "Let's go back."

Nicholas nodded, picking up Martha's reins and bridle. He fitted them neatly around her head and neck, before he retrieved his hammer and helmet from the ground. He placed both back in their place in the bag and on his head respectively, before climbing up Martha's back and into the saddle. He reached a hand down, and took Lady's to pull her up. She leaned against him on the way back.

The world passed by below her in a blur, an almost lovely sight if it wasn't for the added weight holding her down. An emerald shackle. Lady sighed, burying her forehead into Nicholas' back, shoving her scarf up over her mouth to defend from the wind.

How was she going to tell him?

Amadeus did not give her the chance when they returned. Nicholas excused himself to report back to Everett for instructions on cleaning up the corpse and to inform him that their larger dragon troubles were over for now. Martha too, avoided it all by the sheer fact she did not fit inside the house. That left Lady alone with Amadeus.

Whose glare alone could have slain a dragon if given the opportunity.

"I know that you're angry, but I stand by what I did," Lady said, pointing her finger at the man. They were alone in the main sitting room of the house, and the fireplace crackled loudly with a warm and roaring fire. "And after that fight I can say I did the right thing. There was no room for error with that thing."

Amadeus watched her, slouched in the plush armchair that sat by the fire. He had one leg crossed over the other, dressed in a rather elegant evening outfit. With his armor put away, the fine silk shirt and tightly weaved trousers looked ten times more expensive than anything someone in this house could afford. He looked like a king in that chair. Angry, vengeful.

And silent.

Lady crossed her arms, and held her head up high. She was dressed in full armor, and in control of this situation. His angry glaring had no effect on her whatsoever. But she would really appreciate it if he'd say something. Anything. Lady asked, "Nothing to say?"

Amadeus slid one leg off the other and placed both flat on the ground. He dropped his hand on his thigh and licked the side of his lip. Lady remained solid in her place, keeping her arms crossed and her head high. Amadeus stood in a smooth motion that looked like a graceful cat standing, and looked down into her eyes.

"Well?" Lady asked.

Amadeus pushed a loose strand of Lady's hair back behind her ear. He tapped her cheek with the tip of his finger and whispered, "I'm coming with you on the next one."

Lady's heart skipped a beat.

She drew a hand up and held it over her chest where her necklace hung around her neck. Lady flattened her palm over where the stone sat near her breast. A stone the same color as his emerald green eyes— *Emerald!*

"Amadeus, wait!" Lady said, spinning around. He stopped at the door, his hand wrapped around the handle. Lady reached into the bag on her belt and pulled out the much larger emerald necklace, and held it's chain the other hand. "I have something I still need to tell you."

"Yes?" He asked, closing the door again. Amadeus looked at her hands, and the jewelry she held. "Is that Simon's?"

"It is," Lady said. She shuffled over to Amadeus and pulled his hand down. She set the emerald in his palm, closing his fingers around the stone. Lady held it closed and took two heavy breaths to even her voice. "We found it inside the dragon's Hoard Gut."

Amadeus opened his fingers, and turned the pendant over in his palm. He ran his thumb over the word "Simon" engraved onto the back in a steady circle before tracing the letters. Amadeus opened his mouth and closed it tight. He trapped the necklace into a fist and dropped his hand at his side. "The dragon is dead?"

"Very," Lady said, holding her own hands together. Amadeus' eyebrows came together as his face contorted, and he held a hand up to cover his eyes. "Are you going to be okay?"

"Would you mind leaving me for a moment?" He asked, dragging his hand down his face until it covered his mouth. He breathed harder, his chest rising and falling at a worrying rate. "I think I need some time alone."

"Of course," Lady said. She touched his arm, feeling his warm skin under the fabric of his silk shirt. Lady squeezed his arm and let him go. "We're here if you want to talk."

She left the room quietly, and pulled her hair out of its bun as the door clicked closed behind her. Amadeus made a choked sound through the door, and she ran for the back door.

"Ah, so this is where you've been hiding for the past two hours," Nicholas said, taking a seat beside Lady on the roof. He fell on his back and crossed his feet at his ankles, stretching out along the roof tiles. Nicholas watched the sky, pillowing his head in his arms. "You had us a bit worried."

"How'd you know I was up here?" Lady asked, sitting up. She scratched her head, shaking her hair loose around her shoulders.

"A little dragon told me," Nicholas said, holding a hand up and waving down at Martha in the yard. An ultimately useless gesture as she was safe from his coddling under her tarp. Nicholas rolled onto his stomach, dressed down in a plain shirt and trousers. Lady lifted an eyebrow at the edging of his shirt and the threads made tiny vines that climbed up the edges. Maybe his clothes weren't so plain. Nicholas clicked his tongue, and said, "Well, a decent sized dragon anyway. I don't think I'd associate Martha with the word 'little' any time soon, you know?"

Lady peered down over the roof edge, spotting the sliver of space between the tarp and the house. She saw Martha smirking up at her, and she kicked a loose roof tile down at her. The dragon huffed, and Lady moved back to sit on the roof. "You need something?"

"To see how you were," Nicholas said. He pushed up on his elbows and rolled to sit up on the roof's edge. He elbowed Lady lightly in the side. "Wanted to make sure you didn't run off and get yourself into trouble."

Lady grunted.

"Though really I just wanted to figure out where you'd gone to sulk," Nicholas said. "It just sounded more daring that you might run off in a huff."

"Or childish," Lady said. She shook her head and dragged her fingers through her hair. She wrapped it around her fingers and tugged it hard. "How's Amadeus?"

"Fairly well, all considered," Nicholas said. "He came out of his room about ten minutes after we saw you leave through the front door and asked about you."

"Did he?"

"Yes," Nicholas said. He bit the side of his lip, "We said you stepped out and he went back into his room."

"Is he still in there?" Lady asked.

"No," Nicholas said. "He changed clothes into something less fancy and intimidating first, and then came to sit with Everett and I in the dining room."

She huffed and stood up on the top of the roof. *So Amadeus had dressed up on purpose*, Lady thought to herself. *That was just like him.* Lady walked down the side, and grabbed the edge. She dropped down to stand on the ledge of the lower window and crawled back into her room. Nicholas dropped into her room a few steps behind her and brushed off the dirt and dust from his trousers.

"Suppose there's no point in sulking out here if he's already up and about, " Lady said, snapping off the front of her armor. She dumped it on the ground and continued to click off the other pieces. No point in running around in full armor when everyone else had dressed down. She tugged on her undershirt, airing it out a bit. "Everyone have dinner yet?"

Nicholas turned and faced toward the wall, taking the hint as her armor hit the ground. "Yes, but we saved you a plate or two."

Lady swapped out her shirt and pants for a light dress, and tucked her necklace under the neckline. No sense in shining emeralds around him after earlier this evening. Lady kicked off her boots, and tapped Nicholas on the shoulder. "Good."

Nicholas turned and gave Lady a hug and squeezed tight. "Double good."

Lady cleared her throat and he set her down. "You said there was food?"

"There is food," Nicholas said, opening the bedroom door. "Oh, and Lady?"

"Yes?" She asked, adjusting the top of her evening dress.

"Everything is going to be okay," Nicholas said. He reached over and flicked Lady in the cheek with the tip of his fingers. "Amadeus is a big boy, and he'll be fine. So do not worry yourself over it, yes?"

"I'll try not to," Lady said. She slapped Nicholas on the arm and headed out into the hallway. "Let's get food."

"Yes, Ma'am!"

Chapter 11

IN TIME, THE blue bud grew far larger than the ruby roses had predicted, nearing ten times the largest ruby rose's size in as little as two weeks. It was bulbous and bulging, falling over on its side as its precious life inside grew.

The flowers found they would still have to wait, however, as another four full moons passed before the tip of the bud showed signs of opening.

Amadeus took the death of his friend Simon fairly well. Too well, almost. He was quiet for most of the evening, and still deep in thought during breakfast, but by lunch he was helping pack up the carriage (or rather, ordered Drake about to pack up the carriage) as if nothing had happened. A night and a morning had hardly been enough time for a grieving period, surely? Lady had asked once if he was alright, and he had replied with a kind "Yes." She took him at his word, even though something settled uneasily in her stomach with the simple answer.

After breakfast, the trio made one last trip into town to settle accounts and to say goodbye to everyone. Everett and Brianna had thanked and paid both Nicholas and Lady for their services, giving them a blessing as they left. After all of that, Lady was more than ready to get back on the road, but she was pleasantly surprised to see Amadeus had purchased another small bag of candied apples for the trip. He handed them to Lady soon as she left the main doors of City Hall.

"Thank you for bringing me Simon's necklace," he said. Amadeus tapped the side of the bag on his belt, and she heard a slight jingle of the chain inside the leather pouch. He fiddled with the sides of his glove, as they walked, fidgeting in place. "I know that must have been difficult for you, but I appreciate it."

"Then you should probably thank Nicholas," Lady said. She rubbed the back of her neck, before popping another candy piece into her mouth. "He's the one who insisted that we tell you."

Amadeus smiled and shook his head. "I already did."

"Did what?" Lady asked, touching the ground after the last step of stairs. Nicholas was behind her, hugging his cousin and Brianna tightly in the giant bear hugs that she had now learned he was rather famous for all around.

"Thanked Nicholas," Amadeus said. He took one of her candied apples and bit it in half. "I also said he could tag along on our trip to the Lake Dragon if he liked."

When they got back to the house, Lady shoved her bag into the back of Amadeus' carriage, seeing Nicholas' day pack already there. At some point during Lady's two hours of hiding up on the roof, Nicholas had expressed a desire to continue traveling along with Lady and Amadeus. He had no where else to be, and once he heard about their mission to kill the Lake Dragon he was excited to watch or help. So Amadeus had let him.

"Are you going to ride Martha above us?" Lady asked, stepping down and jumping off the edge of the carriage. "Or in the car with us?"

"With you!" Nicholas said. He rolled his shoulders and secured the rest of his bags on Martha's back. He pressed lightly on the side of her neck and loosened her reins. "I'm sure Martha would enjoy a bit of free flying, don't you?"

"Sure she won't fly away?" Lady snorted. She leaned on the carriage and crossed one leg over the other. "What's stopping her from running?"

"Free food and free shiny things," Nicholas said, patting her side. He held his hand up next to his mouth, and mock whispered, "She's quite lazy."

Martha smacked him with her tail, and rolled her eyes. A few ruby scales shed off and she shook herself hard, dropping loose another wave of them. Lady snorted and hopped back up into the carriage. "Whatever you say."

"I'm sure they'll be fine," Amadeus said, already settled on his side of the seat. He had a small book out, and was writing down some notes.

He had Simon's necklace out in his hand and Lady peaked over the edge. "Writing a letter?"

"Yes," Amadeus said. He closed the book and put it aside in a small bag. "But it's nothing important right now. Is everyone ready to go?"

Nicholas popped into the carriage and whistled at the inside. He sat down next to Amadeus, and propped his foot up on the middle row. "I will never get over how big it is in here. What a great way to travel."

"I thought you said 'dragon was the only way' when we were on Martha," Lady asked, leaning back in her seat across from both of the boys. "And you could never go back?"

"Company does wonders," Nicholas said. He held his finger up and swished it back and forth. "And I never said this was better than traveling by dragon, I just said it was a great way to travel."

"Details," Lady said, scrunching her nose. She looked out the window and watched Martha roll her back and yawn. "So she's going to follow us?"

"Yes!" Nicholas said. He leaned back into the seat and stretched out, clearly enjoying the headrest and the pillow-like cushions. Amadeus scooted over an inch, rolling his eyes and sighing. Nicholas answered by leaning toward him more until their shoulders touched, and Lady could see the smirk on Nicholas' face as he crossed his hands over his chest. "Martha will fly high above our heads, but she'll meet us at the town of Drowned Lake."

"If you say so," Lady said. She fell over on her side, making better use of the plush seat. She pulled her legs up on the seat and crossed her hands over her belly. "Wake me when we we get there."

Lady closed her eyes, almost regretting she wouldn't get to see Nicholas and Amadeus fuss at each other for hours. As tempted as it was to watch that show, sleep tugged and pulled at her until Lady passed out on the soft cushions to the sound of her boys bickering under their breaths.

"We're here," Amadeus said, shaking Lady's shoulder. She opened her eyes, and looked up into his and smiled. He tapped her side with the back of his hand and left her vision. "Get up and help us unpack if you want to get dinner on time."

Lady popped up from the carriage seat and stretched. She adjusted her armor, and climbed out of the carriage, her boots sinking an inch into the soft mud that waited outside. She scrunched her nose as she kept walking, her feet squelching and squishing in the wet ground. The closest town to the famed Drowned Lake was home to around twenty thousand people and dirt poor. As such, paving roads or even bothering to do so much as to lay down stones for the paths was either too expensive or too much trouble. Add in the proximity to the marshy lands that surrounded the lake, and you were left with a town of mud.

Drake, bless the man, had already started digging out bedding equipment to throw inside the carriage to make up his makeshift hotel room in the main cab. Their expensive ride was going to attract more attention than Nicholas' dragon in a place like this, amusingly enough. Drake practiced his motions with the same disinterest as he had in both Vineyard Acres and Honey Farms. It amazed her how willing Drake was to sleep in the carriage time and time again instead of the inn with the rest of them. It was moments like these where Lady valued her job as a dragon slayer, and that the only valuables she needed to keep on her could fit in a small pouch at her waist. Drake did it all without complaint, however, and Lady considered that all this meant was he was the right man for the job.

Speaking of the dragon, Nicholas cooed at Martha, encouraging her to land on a rather large boulder off in the distance from the nearest human built structure. The dragon scrunched her nose at the wet ground, shaking her head as if touching it would soil her. *Such a fussy thing, that dragon.*

Lady snorted to herself, ignoring the odd duo for now and dragged her pack out of the back of the carriage. Drake handed her Amadeus' pack without a word, and she rolled her eyes looking around for the man to which it belonged. Spotting him, Lady tracked her way across the mud. Amadeus waited for her by the inn sign post, his traveling cloak bunched up in his hands to avoid touching the ground at all costs.

"I give it two seconds before you start cleaning off your boots once we hit the wooden floors of that inn," Lady said, walking past him and in through the main doors. The lobby was at least clean, save for the mud tracks on the floor of course, though sparsely decorated. A few chairs were spread out across the room here or there, but the main centerpiece was a large long table with equally long benches alongside either side of it. She spotted a bar with drinks to the side, but there wasn't much else. The rack with the keys was also behind the bar, so Lady trotted over to pick out a couple rooms.

Amadeus and Nicholas wouldn't mind sharing.

Lady bit her lip at the thought of the two of them trying to share a room, with the way they pushed and shoved in the carriage, and it was too good of an opportunity not to put it into action. And besides, if Amadeus or Nicholas put up too much of a fuss, one of them could always room with Lady. And if she crossed her fingers hoping it would be the one with black hair and green eyes, well, who could blame her?

"It was three seconds for the record," Amadeus said, leaning over her shoulder and plucking one of the keys out of her hand. She looked down, and sure enough his boots were spotless, as if they had never so much as heard of the word "mud" in their lives. Amadeus threw a cheeky grin at her, and said "Does that mean you're paying for the rooms tonight?"

Lady could play that game, and put the money down on the bar top. She grabbed the other key from the attendant and said, "For the week."

Amadeus laughed, a sound Lady had found herself missing very much, and walked past her to the stairs. He looked at the room key and the tag on it as he ascended the stairs, and Lady paid for a drink while she was there.

She might need it.

Nicholas came into the room a moment later, the mud up to his knees on his armor. There were splashes of it higher, as if he had attempted to avoid a wrestling match in the mud and only succeeded halfway. He grumbled under his breath and threw his hands in the air. "That dragon is impossible some days."

"Martha doesn't like mud?" Lady asked, turning and leaning on the bar. She ignored the slight jolt of the bartender at Nicholas' mention of the word "dragon" but was glad he didn't question it. Lady sipped her drink as Nicholas sloshed over, adding to the already dirty floor. "Odd for a creature that lives outside most of her life."

"Do you enjoy mud?" Nicholas asked, he hopped up onto a bar stool, and grabbed the counter as it wobbled. He steadied himself until the stool stopped moving, and pressed his boot on the floor to keep it that way. "But honestly, I can't bring her into such a small town, and I don't have enough tarp to line the ground for her."

The bartender, and possibly inn owner, cleared his throat next to Nicholas. A sheepish smile appeared on the dragon rider's face, and he placed a few coins on the table and ordered a drink. That seemed to appease the stout man, and he left only to return a few moments later with a full pint.

"Mud washes off," Nicholas said. He pulled the warm drink closer and muttered, "You'd think she'd never heard of a bath before!"

"Oh yes, who doesn't love a night sleeping out in the mud all night just to wash it off later?" Lady asked. She held her hand in her cheek, and sipped her beer. "What could her problem be?"

"Point," Nicholas said. He rubbed the back of his neck and drank heavily from the beer he had ordered. He yawned loudly, ruffling his curly brown hair. Nicholas sipped from his glass. "Maybe I should camp out with her. She would hardly have the right to complain if I do that."

"I would suggest that, but I've already paid for three guests, so you'll just have to suffer," Lady said, shaking the second room key in the air.

"If you insist," Nicholas said, though his voice sounded more relieved than argumentative. Nicholas drank, humming to himself deep in thought. "I'll just have to get her something nice as a favor."

"Yes, spoil her more," Lady said. She was surprised Martha was still in good shape with all the pampering she'd seen. That first dominant display back in Honey Farms must have been for show. The longer she hung around Nicholas and Martha, the more obvious it was just who had who whipped. Lady flicked Nicholas in the side of the head. "That's exactly what she needs."

"I think I shall," Nicholas said, ignoring her tone. He tapped his glass against Lady's in a fake toast. "But at the end of the day, the happier Martha is, the happier I am."

"You make it sound like she's your wife instead of your steed," Lady said, snorting at the analogy. "Unless you two get up to things you don't tell me about?"

"Hardly," Nicholas said, snorting at the absurdity of Lady's joke. He finished off his beer and slammed the glass hard on the counter in good cheer. He took a peek at Lady's room key number before snatching it up. He saluted her, tossing the key up into the air before catching it. "I'll see you later this evening at dinner, yes?"

Lady sipped her beer as he trotted upstairs. If Amadeus took one key, and Nicholas took the other, that meant that Lady got to pick who she shared with. There were two beds in each room, so it'd hardly be any different than before. Not indecent in the slightest bit.

She smiled into her glass.

As if there was any question as to who she'd pick.

"You would not believe it!" Nicholas said, taking a seat on the long bench next to Lady. He straddled it, leaning one elbow on the table and throwing the other arm out toward the open room in an excited gesture. "There's going to be a big party tonight!"

"A party?" Amadeus asked, seated across the table on a particularly rickety portion of the bench. Every so often, he'd grab the table to keep the seat from moving under him, and Lady tried not to giggle each time. He picked at his plate of porridge and took a mouthful of the bland Inn Special. "What sort of party?"

"A big one up at the main hall of the town," Nicholas said. He crossed both arms on the table, and snuck a piece of cheese off of Lady's full plate. Nicholas popped it into his mouth and tapped on the table. "I heard it from my room neighbor. Apparently some rich guy donated a lot of money to make a nice party hall downtown, go figure why, and every couple of weeks he throws a well-to-do to show it off. Anyone can come as long as they can afford the entrance fee."

"Sounds boring," Lady said, sliding her plate out of Nicholas' reach. The only one who could steal food from plates around here was her! She guarded her food, only revealing it from the safety of her arms to eat a few bites herself. "A bunch of rich people standing around and talking about the same things week after week. What's the fun in that?"

"Polite conversation, good food and a bit of dancing," Amadeus said, swirling around his porridge. He dropped the spoon in the dish and shoved it toward Nicholas, who took the bowl happily. Amadeus talked while Nicholas finished off his food. "It can be quite enjoyable if you're dressed properly and know how to work a room."

"See? We've got it right from our own residential rich boy: Boring," Lady said, dragging out the last word.

"Would you mind if I proved you wrong?" Amadeus asked. He folded his hands on the table, leaning forward with one eyebrow raised in challenge. "Or at the very least give me the opportunity to attempt to do so?"

"And how do you plan to do that?" Lady asked right back at him.

"Would you give me the privilege of escorting you to the party as my date?" Amadeus asked, reaching across the table. He took her hand and kissed the knuckles. "I know you have a dress to wear, courtesy of Miss Agatha."

Lady rolled their hands over, and scrunched her nose. "I'm afraid I left that lovely thing back at her house in Vineyard Acres. Such a shame."

"You left the green one behind," Amadeus said, putting her hand on the table and patting her knuckles. His expression grew more amused by the second, and it created a brand new and even more awful nest of butterflies in Lady's stomach. "But I have a lovely red one packed and ready to go that Agatha snuck into my belongings for just such an occasion. She said you're always horribly unprepared for these things."

"Prepared enough to hit her next time I see her," Lady said under her breath. She stabbed a block of cheese. "And what if something happens? I don't know if you've noticed, but dragon attacks are rather common and I am a Dragon Slayer. It's my duty to be prepared at all times."

"Martha and I can handle it," Nicholas said, welcoming a second plate of porridge and cheese from the waitress. He pushed aside Amadeus' empty dish, and stared at the new bowl as it was set on the table and inhaled the home-cooked, though still very bland, meal. "You have a fun night off, and we will watch the town."

"There you go," Amadeus said, pointing his finger at Nicholas. "Someone to cover your duties for you, while you have a night out. So what do you say? Care to join me?"

Lady looked away from those green eyes, and pushed away from the table. "Then I suppose I better get dressed."

"Lady," Amadeus asked.

"Yes?"

"That's what I wanted," Amadeus said. He stood and kissed her hand across the table again, this time lingering on her knuckles with a sly smirk befitting a rich, spoiled brat. "Never take out a lady until she says 'yes' completely. Now if you'll excuse me, I should probably start getting ready myself as we're already fashionably late."

Lady shouted, "That didn't count!" after him up the stairs.

Chapter 12

THE BUD BLOOMED under the light of a full moon.

The ruby roses gathered around it as the petals peeled away from the rounded shape. In the center in a puff of pollen, was a small fleshy ball. The small child had curled up tight in itself, shivering with the removal of the petal blanket. The roses watched in a hush quiet, but the little one did not move.

A spectating bird landed on the side petal and decided to give the little one a push with a gentle peck to its side. The child rolled over, revealing a face and four limbs with tiny hands and feet.

It was a little girl, perfectly formed and perfectly human.

The ruby roses let out a great shout for joy, filling the valley with the musical sounds of their petals shaking and scraping against each other.

The baby giggled at the sound, clapping in instinct for the beautiful music.

The looming community center was unwelcome and out of place in this impoverished town.

The tall clean building was a mismatch to the crumbling ones around it, and the many gardens and greenery that surrounded it were almost an insult to the famous town mud. It was a lavish building with marble floors, fine art on display around every corner, and smooth walls made of a material that Lady did not know the name. Her shoes clicked on the marble tiles as she entered the lobby on Amadeus' arm, and shivered at the chill that came from the room.

Amadeus paid for their entry with ease, securing a welcoming atmosphere by tipping the doorman, and they blended right in with the rest of the obnoxiously richly dressed patrons in the room.

For the occasion, Amadeus had shed his armor and evening clothes. He replaced them with a fresh ensemble that consisted of a rich red dress jacket, complete with a neatly pressed black silk blouse underneath. A darker red vest hid behind the jacket, shaping his slim form to perfection. Even his dark boots looked rich over his black trousers. How he found a jacket to match her dress on such short notice was suspicious, and that suspicion's name was the matchmaking Agatha. However meddling the gem store owner was, even Lady had to admit they did look like quite the pair.

Lady twirled a curl of hair around her finger, loose strands of it hanging from the bun Nicholas had placed on her head. They covered the clean side of her face, leaving the scarred side open to the air at her request. Lady gathered a turned head here or there at the sight, but most of them were too busy gossiping about how lovely she and Amadeus looked as a matching set to care.

She wasn't sure if that was comforting or not.

"You look lovely this evening," Amadeus said, walking her down the stairs to the main floor. His body was warm, and Lady found herself naturally leaning into it to hide from the cold of the room. He spoke softly, almost whispering to keep away the prying ears that tried to muscle in on their conversations for new gossip. "I don't believe I got a chance to tell you earlier at the inn."

As Amadeus had said earlier, Agatha had smuggled into his bags a dress in Lady's size for a formal occasion. It had a high collar that didn't get in the way of her emerald necklace, long sleeves, and rich velvety red fabric that trailed behind her on the ground. The entire dress was decorated in finely embroidered roses that gave the fabric a unique texture, that just so happened to match the same embroidered pattern on Amadeus' vest. Agatha was quite the planner, but Lady took great satisfaction in knowing there was a stain of mud on the underskirt to spite her.

But, Lady smoothed down the fabric under her hands, it really was lovely. And again, she might owe Agatha a small bit of thanks for the assistance.

"I believe you did," Lady said squeezing his arm, "But as I've said before, a woman always loves a proper compliment."

Amadeus squeezed her arm. "Then I'm happy that I managed to give you a proper one."

A serving man with a tray full of drinks in glass flutes walked by, stopping to allow Lady and Amadeus to each take one drink. She sipped it, and the bubbly liquid felt wonderful on her tongue. It was a light taste, and instincts told her it must have cost a fortune. She looked around the room at all the finely dressed people, laughing and covered in jewelry.

"I don't think a single person at this party lives in this town," Lady said. She sipped her drink, and loosened her hold on Amadeus' arm. "What's the fun in this again?"

"Extravagance is a bit of an acquired taste, I must admit," Amadeus said. He had yet to touch his drink, and merely held it in his hand. Amadeus tugged on her arm and led them to the other side of the room where giant tables full of food were set out. "Most of the fun is forgetting about everyone else in the world for a few hours."

"That doesn't sound healthy," Lady said. She let go of his arm and passed the table of food to stop at the window. She pushed aside the plush curtain, and glanced outside at the dark gardens. Just beyond the fence, she could see the rooftops of the town. "Especially when the rest of the world is right out there, in homes that are falling apart and cold porridge for dinner."

Amadeus stepped behind her, handing her a made up plate full of candied cherries, caramel drizzled apple slices, and two large chunks of chocolate. She took the plate, letting the curtain fall closed behind her. Lady ate a cherry, nearly groaned at the sugary perfection, and immediately rolled her eyes at his smiling face. "Though I can see how easy it can be when you have luxury shoved right under your nose."

"As true as that is, you do have a point," Amadeus said. He sipped his drink and led Lady easily around the room, weaving in and out of laughing guests that spoke of years of practice. Nicholas navigated city streets like a pro, but this was Amadeus' ring of expertise. He glided along, welcome and in control. The other attendees moved out of his way as he passed as if they could feel the aura of nobility on him. "And it's sometimes nice to remind ourselves that this luxury is something we must work for to keep, and share as often as possible to do so."

"And what sharing have you done lately?" Lady asked, smiling a bit as she bit a cherry off its stem.

"A gentleman never tells his charitable efforts," Amadeus said. "Or else it's no longer an act of charity, but one of vanity."

Amadeus leaned in and whispered next to her ear, "And vanity is something of which I already have trouble controlling. Why add to it?"

Lady bit into a piece of chocolate. "I wouldn't."

"Then maybe I won't," Amadeus said. He took her hand and led her away with from the tables with a smile. "Come now, there's still quite a bit to see."

There was one event that Lady had forgotten about when she spoke of boring rich parties: The dancing.

"You are unfairly good at a lot of things," Lady said, allowing herself to be spun around in the center of the floor. Her dress opened into a red halo, the folds in the fabric resembling a giant rose as she turned. Amadeus took hold of her waist and continued the steps of the waltz with ease. "Business, fine conversation, and dancing, too? Is there anything you're bad at?"

"I'm not very good at cooking, I'm afraid," Amadeus said. He turned the both of them in time with the music, following along with the other people dancing in a giant circle in the room. The music was light and upbeat, and so were his feet. Lady giggled, following along as well as she could remember. Amadeus said, "I tend to burn everything to a crisp."

"One tick mark against you," Lady said, leaning up close. "Hardly matters when you've got an entire checklist of good things."

"I imagine you'd find more marks the more you got to know me," Amadeus said. The music stopped and so did they, pausing in the middle of the room. The small orchestra began a new song, one much slower and sweeter, and they danced again to match. Amadeus began again with smooth and even steps, gently leading Lady along by the hand. "I'm good at hiding them from company."

"I really don't know you all that well, do I?" Lady asked. She tossed her hair over her shoulder to see his face better through her good eye. "Even after all this time, I still mostly know that you deal in gemstones and are a bit obsessed with cleanliness."

"Not much else to me after that," Amadeus laughed. He squeezed her hand, and tugged them both forward to the side. "Unless you want the nitty gritty details, such as I live with the King in the main castle of Ruby Mines, and being from the First Family I have quite a few social obligations. But I think you'd find most of that boring, wouldn't you?"

"Not too horribly boring," Lady said. She squeezed his hand right back. "Or at least I feel you can make it more interesting."

"If we're being honest," Amadeus said, "I think I know even less about you than you know about me. You slay dragons and you are concerned for the safety of others. I'm not sure what else there is to you."

"Is that all you know about me?" Lady asked. She leaned forward and bumped into him with her elbow. "After all this time? I'm crushed."

"You love food," he said, stopping them both. Amadeus huffed, and waved at the food tables in the distance. "How could I possibly have forgotten that?"

"I have no idea," Lady said. They both walked back into the crowd, Lady smoothing down her dress from it's new ruffles. "It's only the first thing you learned about me."

"No, the first thing I learned about you is that you hate dragons," Amadeus said, standing a bit straighter as he headed toward the back room. "And that you like flowers."

"I don't believe I said that," Lady said.

Amadeus tapped a rosette embroidered on the shoulder of her dress. "You didn't need to."

The moon hung low in the sky over their heads, beautiful and full. Lady sat on the metal bench, her legs tucked under it with a cup of warm wine in her hands. Amadeus sat next to her, sipping the red drink. Surrounded by roses and all sorts of flowers in the back garden, the atmosphere was made perfect with the lights from the ballroom creating a warm glow over the area nearest to the building. Bathed in soft blue moonlight, the rest of the garden carried a heavenly sweetness that made the company and wine more pleasant.

"There is one thing, that I've been curious about for quite some time," Amadeus said, wrapping an arm around the back of the bench. He tucked Lady into his side, and she was more than happy to allow it. Amadeus tapped his finger on her shoulder, the touch light and hand warm. "If you would indulge a question?"

"I suppose that depends on what you ask," Lady said, reclining so that her back touched his arm. "What did you want to know?"

"Your name," he said. Lady leaned into him, and he dropped his arm around her shoulder properly. "It's rather uncommon, and I was wondering if it had any special meaning. I've been rather curious since we met."

"Uncommon," Lady smiled into her cup. She tilted her head back and downed the rest of the cup. "Odd you mean. Who names a little girl 'Lady?' It's rather boring."

"Your parents, as it would seem," Amadeus said. "Does it have special meaning? Or were they just uncreative?"

Lady set her empty glass on the bench and rested her head on his shoulder. She inhaled the smell of the flowers around her, and the scent of cinnamon coming from Amadeus' coat. "I was named after my father's favorite fairy tale."

Amadeus squeezed her shoulder. The encouraging look in his eyes drew knots in Lady's stomach. She leaned toward him, closing her eyes and remembering the details.

"It was called 'Lady of the Roses' and he read it to me at least once a week before bed when I was little. I think he loved reading it as much as I enjoyed listening to it. My father always enjoyed himself, sometimes changing his voice to match the characters," Lady said, plucking at a ruffle on her dress. "Often times he'd read it twice a week if I asked, but no more than that. He said 'Special things should be for special times.' It was ours. A short, silly little tale about flowers wanting to be loved."

Amadeus pulled a rose off the side of a bush and handed it to her. Lady turned the flower over in her fingers, the red petals clear even in the dim light. She kissed the edge of the petals and let her hands fall into her lap.

"The party was boring, as predicted," Lady said, mumbling into his chest. She reached down and rubbed his thigh once, letting her hand rest there in an odd moment of bravery. "But this part of it's quite alright."

"I was just thinking the same," he said, resting his cheek on her hair. His voice was a whisper, only for Lady and Lady alone. "I couldn't think of anything in there that is better than being out here alone."

Amadeus reached up and pulled out her bun, letting her hair fall around her shoulders. He fluffed it out with his fingers, loosening the strands. Lady smiled, breathing deeply. She turned the flower in her hand, and bit the side of her lip.

"Amadeus," she said.

"Yes?"

"When we get back to the inn, I was wondering," Lady said, she shifted, sitting up but still pressed against him. Her heart beat hard under her breast, driven by fear and anticipation. "If you wouldn't mind—"

The roar sounded across the entire garden, a screeching cry that had Lady reaching up to cover her ears. A wind passed them, and she jumped to her feet as it passed. The shadow was long and large, maybe twice Martha's size. The outline in the dark was difficult to see, but it was definitely a dragon with four legs and a swarm of horns on it's head and back. It passed by the community building and headed toward the center of town.

"Shit," Lady hissed, she gathered up her skirts and made for the marble steps that led back to the ballroom. "I need to go he—"

Amadeus grabbed her hand and yanked her to a halt, cutting off her words and her travel. Lady tugged on her arm, but his grip was steel and had a strength she didn't think his slim form was capable of having.

"Let go," Lady said. She twisted her arm, but he held tight. "I need to go after that before it hurts someone!"

"It was a medium sized dragon at best, and the scales weren't even of a gemstone or we would have seen it glittering," Amadeus said. He let go of Lady's wrist, but swapped it for holding her shoulders. "Nicholas can handle it."

"What if he needs help?" Lady asked, pushing at his chest a bit.

"You're taking a night off, remember? You agreed to it yourself that you'd let Nicholas take care of any dragon attacks tonight," Amadeus said. His grip tightened on her shoulders, and his eyes burned as they locked with hers. "Stay here, and stay with me."

"But the dragon," Lady insisted, turning away and looking into the far sky where the dragon had gone. Every inch of her rushed to go after it. Amadeus' fingers burned her shoulders where they held her locked in place. Lady twisted in the grip. "I need to go."

"Do you trust Nicholas?"

"What?" Lady asked, cowed by his tone.

Amadeus' expression was stone as he whispered, "Do you trust Nicholas or not?"

"I," Lady said. She shook her head and reached up to touch her temple. "Of course I do, but that's not the point."

"It is the point," Amadeus said. He touched her cheek and pressed their foreheads together. Amadeus reached up with both hands, holding her face so that his fingers rested on the back of her neck. Their noses knocked, and she could feel his heated breath. "You are not the only dragon slayer in the world, and you are hardly responsible for hunting down and killing every last one you see. Trust Nicholas, and let him handle it tonight."

"But." Lady bit her lip. She leaned against him, reaching up to hold onto his wrists even as her stomach twisted. Lady trembled in his hold, her breath heavy and her heart racing. He wasn't wrong. No matter how she hated it, Amadeus wasn't wrong. She whispered, "Okay, I will trust him. I'll trust Nicholas."

A second roar entered the night, though this one more familiar. Lady and Amadeus both turned to watch a flash of red dash by the sky. It followed after the larger dragon, and Lady grabbed Amadeus' arm. She dug her nails into the sleeve and watched fire light up in the sky, far in the distance.

"See? He's already taking care of it," Amadeus said. He drew his fingers through her hair and fluffed it out again. "Let's sit back down."

Lady let Amadeus lead her back to the bench. She sat, her back to the action behind her. She stared at the starry sky to the front, and leaned on the cold iron back of the bench. Lady picked up her rose, and squeezed the stem hard in her hands.

"There was something you were going to ask before we were interrupted," Amadeus said, standing next to the bench. "Was that right?"

"It was nothing," Lady said, ripping a petal off the side of her rose.

Amadeus rested a hand on his waist. "Of course."

Despite the sounds of battle behind them, the rest of the night was far too quiet. Lady longed for her cheap bed at the inn, and to get out of this dress.

Chapter 13

THE BABY FROM the witch's blue flower grew as children did in the rest of human society. A small helpless thing from birth until she was old enough to listen to the rose's lessons. Many living creatures in the valley came to aid the young one's growth. The birds brought her food, and the squirrels and insects were her friends.

Though first and foremost, the child always came back to the roses that she loved.

The little creature adored her rose guardians, and always laughed and giggled at everything they did in total amusement. She petted their petals, and stroked around the thorns of their stems. When her words came, she spoke of her love.

There was no fear or reason for sorrow, only adoration.

The little girl loved them, and they loved she. For many years they raised her there alone, until she was no longer a little child, and showed signs of growing into a young woman.

Lady had roomed with Nicholas that night.

She wasn't exactly angry with Amadeus after stopping her from going after that dragon, but she wasn't exactly happy with him either. Something had felt off about the encounter, and Lady felt it best to be alone for a while to sort out her thoughts. If only she could tell what was bothering her so much about last night, perhaps she could take steps to fix it.

What had been so wrong?

Was it that he stopped her from going? How tightly he had grabbed her arm, or the steel in his voice when he practically ordered her to stay put? Lady bit her lip. Was it that he doubted her trust in Nicholas, or was she angry that he'd been right and she didn't know how to leave well enough alone when it came to dragons?

Lady pulled on her shirt, rubbing her fingers against the pendant that sat on her chest. No, she wasn't angry about that. Couldn't be about any of that. Agatha had always teased her that at the first sign of a dragon she went running. Wasn't last night even more proof? Amadeus hadn't been wrong, though he could have been less blunt about it.

She really wasn't out to kill every dragon in the world.

Just the one.

Maybe she was just angry that he disagreed with her, right or not. Lady huffed and tugged on her armor piece by piece as she dressed. It wasn't often other people ordered her around that way with such authority. Who did he think he was to declare what she should and shouldn't do?

Nicholas snored to her side, sprawled out on the second bed unaware of her internal struggles. Lady sat on hers and pulled on her boots. She paused, buckling the last strap. Amadeus had been right about that, too, if she admitted it.

Lady hadn't trusted Nicholas to handle things.

She knew that he was capable enough to handle it, but had immediately assumed he needed help the second she spotted the dragon in the sky.

There was no trust there.

And Nicholas had handled it fine without her. When Lady and Amadeus got back from the party, he was already sitting victorious with the head of the dragon in the middle of the inn's lobby. How they'd gotten it in through the small door, she had no idea, but the owner was quite happy to have such an amazing trophy to show off and gather customers to gawk.

"Martha's quite happy, too," Nicholas had said. He smacked the dead dragon's horn with a laugh. "This beastie barely had a hoard to share with her, but there were some lovely trinkets."

Lady nodded at him in congratulations, and passed right on by to her room to change and pass out in her bed. She had tried to dream, but all she could think about was Amadeus and how he had looked when he asked her to stay with him.

She grabbed her sword and placed it with her other belongings. Full in armor, she walked over and shoved Nicholas off his bed. He struggled from his blanket cocoon on the floor and she shouted, "Get up!" as she left.

"Did you have a good night?" Amadeus asked, leaning on the wall across from her door. He had a book open and looked rather dapper reading while dressed in that shining silver armor of his. "You seemed rather tired when we got back."

"Well enough," Lady said. She snapped his book closed and took it from him. "I did want to have a word with you, though."

"Oh?" Amadeus asked, following her. She stomped down the stairs, shoving his book in her belt. Lady braided her hair as she went, and pulled it up into a bun on her head by the time she hit the bottom stair. A routine she had well practiced. "You're not coming this evening when Nicholas and I go after the Lake Dragon."

"I could have sworn that I made it clear that I was indeed going with you," Amadeus said, straightening his gloves. He walked with Lady to the main table and sat next to the dead dragon head. Even with attempts to cover it up, the rotten smell was near overwhelming. Amadeus did not seem to mind and continued with his stubbornness. "Whether you want me there or not. I'm not letting you two go alone again."

Lady did not sit as she approached, keeping her upper ground as she stood next to him. "Do you trust me?"

"Excuse me?"

"Last night you asked if I trusted Nicholas to handle the situation and to sit out the battle," Lady said, gripping her hand into a fist. She held her shoulders back and head high. "Now I'm asking you: Do you trust me?"

"I do," Amadeus said, resting his arm on the table.

"Then do you trust that I can handle it?" Lady said, leaning over to talk with him face to face. "And do you trust that I know what I'm talking about when I say that you'll get in the way?"

Amadeus paused for a full moment, before blinking slowly. He sighed deeply, covering his eyes. Lady held her breath waiting for the answer as his body stilled. Amadeus smacked the table after a few heavy breaths, and rubbed his eyes with his fingers. "I do."

"Good," Lady said, releasing a breath. She sat down on the bench, and pat his arm. "I'm glad that's settled."

"Yes," he answered. Amadeus pulled his hand down and rested both on the table. "When do you leave?"

"Right after lunch," Lady said, relaxing her shoulders. She nudged his arm with her elbow. "Nicholas and I worked out the details last night when he got in and readied for bed. We'll leave at noon, and after you tell us exactly where its lair is, we'll stake it out for weak points."

"And then?"

"We'll come back here and make a more proper plan once we know the layout of its lair better." Lady waved down a server and gave a large order, paying double what it was worth. "We'll take it down while it sleeps."

"I wish you the best of luck with that," Amadeus said, voice quiet. "I really do."

"We won't need luck," Lady said. She put her hand on his shoulder and squeezed, feeling the armor under her hands. "Just your faith that we'll come home."

"I'll wish it for you both," Amadeus said, something odd in his voice that Lady couldn't place. Something strained and almost desperate. Amadeus leaned in close, their noses brushing as he whispered, "Because you will need it."

"Wonderful," Nicholas said, throwing his hands in the air. He and Lady stood about three inches deep in the sinking mud as Martha hissed and flapped her wings hard in the air. She hadn't flown away, but she was most definitely not landing. "You manage to convince Amadeus to stay at the hotel for the rest of the night, and I can't seem to get Martha to leave."

"What seems to be the trouble?" Lady asked. The idea of renting a couple horses and leaving the blasted dragon behind was sounding better and better. "You forget to give her a necklace from last night's dead dragon?"

Nicholas threw his hands in the air. "She was all perfectly fine up until I told her where we were going. Then she goes and throws a fit up there."

"You don't think she knows the dragon we're going after, do you?" Lady asked. She crossed her arms and laughed. "Maybe she's just scared."

Martha screeched through her reins, and sucked in a hissed breath. The dragon dropped into the mud, splashing Nicholas and Lady both with a wave of the thick muck. She shook her shoulders hard, and her body contorted. Lady drew her sword stepping back, and Nicholas stared. Martha ripped her bridle free, releasing an agonizing shriek of pain from the transformation. Nicholas walked forward a few steps, with his hand reached out as if he wanted to comfort her. Martha's body shook and shrunk until the figure of a woman stood in the mud in her place.

"You better believe I'm terrified!" Martha's human form practically roared, voice contorted by still forming vocal chords. She stomped through the mud, her packs and saddles dumped behind and sinking in the mud. Martha's human form had wild, long red hair that framed a dark face with fierce blue eyes. Her teeth were sharp and snarling, with loose scales still clinging to her cheeks and body in random places in her half, unfinished transformation. "You're going after the Heart of the Drowned Lake!"

"Martha! You're human!" Nicholas exclaimed, pointing his finger at her. He slapped his palm over his eyes, and took a step back. "And naked! How long have you been able to do that!?"

"The entire time, you idiot. All dragons can do it, but who wants to be like this?" Martha winced gesturing down at herself. She tugged at her red hair, and scrunched her nose. "All soft and defenseless. It's wretched."

Nicholas sloshed through the mud, looking through two of his fingers without taking his hand down, and yanked a blanket out of the pack. He handed it to her, and she wrapped it around her shoulders to humor him. Nicholas pulled his hand down and, still gaping, asked, "Why haven't you ever done it before?"

"I had nothing to say!" Martha shrieked. She shoved Nicholas into the mud, right on his back. She stomped her foot in-between his legs and growled. "But now I do! You two have lost your minds if you think you can challenge that dragon. He is a Great Dragon! The biggest and most terrifying of all of us!"

"Now let me say something," Lady hissed, shoving Martha's shoulder to turn the other woman. "If I can't defeat this dragon, then there's no way I'll be able to kill the Obsidian of Ruby."

"The Obsidian of Ruby?" Martha asked, snickering with a cruel, mocking laugh. She got up close, near nose to nose with Lady and blew a puff of hot air in her face. Martha growled with a knowing smirk that looked wrong on the half-human face. "That is the truest thing that you have ever said, and I'll let you in on a little secret: You can't kill the Lake Dragon."

"I can," Lady said, grabbing the blanket wrapped around Martha's shoulders. "And you're not only going to watch me, but you're also going to take me there."

"I'll take you there," Martha said, "But you're on your own from that point. Nicholas and I aren't helping you die."

"Martha," Nicholas said, coming up next to them. "Come now, we have to help."

"The only thing that waits for you on this trip is death," Martha said, shoving Nicholas back down into the mud with ease. She poked Lady in the shoulder, pouting in her anger. "I'm not letting my meal ticket kick the bucket."

"Lady, I have a feeling that she might be serious," Nicholas said, sitting up on his elbows in the mud. He flicked a chunk of mud off his hand, and sighed. "I might have trouble helping you if she insists on interfering."

"That's alright, Nicholas," Lady said. She narrowed her eyes, and sucked in a breath. "I can do it alone. A ride's all I need."

"I'm sure she'll change her mind if you need an escort out," Nicholas said. He rubbed his hands together. "I'm sure we can help at least that much."

Lady glared at the uncooperative dragon wench, and hissed, "Here's hoping I won't need it."

Martha transformed back into her dragon form without another word. Nicholas reattached her bags and bridle with shaking hands and constant glances between the dragon's face and what he was doing. Seeing Martha as a human unnerved him far more than Lady realized. Nicholas eventually pulled himself up into the saddle, and Lady hopped up on her back, equally silent. Their trip to the far corner of the Drowned Lake was quiet and tense in a way that she had been hoping to avoid.

Lady hoped Amadeus was having a much better time back at the room reading and catching up on his letters. Perhaps he'd gone out to the carriage to order around Drake in boredom. Lady shook her head. It didn't matter what he was doing back at the inn when she had her own job to do!

"We're almost to the place Amadeus pointed out on the map," Nicholas whispered, as if he were scared to speak too loud and be heard. The statement brought Lady fully into the present and she leaned in close to hear him better. Nicholas asked, "How did he know this was where the dragon's main hoard was, anyway?"

"Businessmen have better information networks than we do," Lady answered. She searched the murky and watery ground for a good landing place. "Go figure."

Martha found a spot to land before Lady did, and dumped both her and Nicholas onto the ground next to the boulder she sat on with the rough landing. Instead of mud, they were knee deep in water from the marsh that surrounded the lake's edge. Everything smelled like salt and fish, and Lady pulled up a scarf to cover her nose.

The sun set in the distance, their day light escaping all the faster after their delayed start. Their sources indicated that this particular beast was nocturnal, and the last thing Lady wanted was to fight a dragon that size in the dark. She rubbed the back of her neck and turned to Nicholas. "We might have to change up our plans. Just a quick scout today, and come back tomorrow morning for a real search."

"I can work with that," Nicholas said, swallowing and backing up to stand next to Martha. "If that's the case, I shall help you."

Martha grabbed the back of his armor with her claws and dragged him up onto the boulder, dumping him on his stomach. She sat on him.

"Or perhaps I will be waiting here for you when you get back," he gasped, thankful his armor protected his soft insides from her weight. "Good luck!"

Lady didn't mind Martha's over protectiveness as much as she thought she would, and waded through the marsh toward the lake. Just to the far left, there should be a large opening about the size of the community center in the town. It connected to a pit carved out of the thick clay and rock beneath the water where the dragon stored all of its treasures, and made its home.

If the dragon was asleep, there shouldn't be too much of an issue sneaking up on it and stabbing it in the neck. It was only when they were awake that Great Dragons were such a horrific and horrible threat. However, the dragon was aware of that, too. Why else would it make its den under the water and far from sight? Getting to the dragon was almost more trouble than finding it while it was awake.

Lady trod carefully, making sure not to overstep and fall into the deeper parts of the marsh. Her thrashing would wake up everything in the area and ruin the whole stealth part of her scouting mission. Lady needed two things: To find the exact location of the entrance, and secondly, to find a way down that didn't involve drowning.

Should be a piece of cake.

Lady approached a darkened area of the marsh, close to the edge of a nearby lake. Watching each footstep, careful of any sudden drops, she pushed aside the tall grass. Lady smiled at the giant black spot in the water, and knelt near the edge. Though the light was leaving, she caught a glimpse of something sparkling near the side of the deposit. She reached for it, and pulled free a small gold chain that must have gotten misplaced or moved on accident during an exit or entrance from the lair. Lady squeezed the necklace tight, whispering, "Looks like I found my entrance."

On the horizon the sun dropped just below the surface and she shifted in place. There was no question that they'd done enough for today. With the light gone, it was time for Lady to make a swift exit and regroup with the new information. There was no point in continuing now when she could barely see a thing as it was and it was only sure to grow darker as time passed.

A bubble popped on the water's surface near her knee. Lady leaned over the edge of the black pool and looked down to greet a bright pair of milky white eyes glowing in the dark water.

Lady sprinted in the other direction back toward Martha.

Water splashed around her from the movement and the mud clung to her feet, slowing every step. A monstrous clawed paw slammed into the marsh grass beside her, the fat arm next to it covered in thick barnacles and shells so dense she couldn't even tell what his scales could be made of underneath it all. Lady kept running, only to look over her shoulder and confirm that the Heart of the Drowned Lake was every bit the giant she'd been told.

The beast towered over everything like a mountain, and he had only crawled halfway out of his lair.

Lady ran faster, fighting the water and grass with every step as she headed for the boulder. She would listen to every single "I told you so" that was given if she got away from that beast in one piece. There was no way she could fight it hand to hand like this. The ground shook as it lumbered behind her. Each footstep felt like an earthquake. Lady always knew one-on-one was never an option. That was why they were trying to catch it asleep! The beast roared behind her and she ran faster. Lady shoved grass out of her way and kept moving. She looked around frantically for the boulder where she'd left Martha and Nicholas. They had to be here somewhere!

A harsh and sudden wind burst through the air, that drew both Lady and the crawling giant to a stop. The air whistled, and Lady hissed as something flew past her face. She grabbed her cheek and drew her fingers back covered in blood from a cut. The dragon behind her had covered itself with his giant wings and was hissing at the sky. A small object glittered in the grass at her feet, and Lady reached down to touch it.

Her hands shook as she picked up the piece of volcanic glass.
Obsidian.

Chapter 14

THE ROSES ADORED their little princess, and her place among them. She was the light of their lives, and her adoration of their beautiful forms made her all the more special.

The ruby roses could not even remember a time that existed before she arrived, and they did not wish to.

Martha plucked Lady from the ground with her claws, and she was dragged up onto the dragon's back by a frantic Nicholas. Shaking, she clung to Nicholas as he helped her up into the saddle. Roars and shrieks filled the air around them, as loud as thunder. Lady held the piece of obsidian in her hand so tightly that her palms bled through the gloves as its edges sliced through the fabric.

"Thought you might want a ride out of there," Nicholas said, as Martha flew higher and farther away from the two large dragons. Lady trembled hard enough that her armor rattled. Nicholas kept his voice low and soothing as he tacked on, "Especially when that second one showed up."

"The Obsidian of Ruby," Lady whispered, leaning over the side of Martha as far as she could to see down below. The obsidian dragon from her nightmares had appeared in the flesh, with eyes of red burning brighter than the fire from its mouth. Lady clutched tightly to Nicholas' arm, and watched in awe as the two dragons battled down below. "Why is it here?"

"To pick a fight with our Lake Dragon, it seems," Nicholas said, holding onto one of Martha's horns as they both leaned over her side to see beyond the pounding wings. Nicholas trembled under her hold, watching intensely. "He seems rather angry."

Nicholas was not far from the truth.

The Obsidian of Ruby was a force to be reckoned with, even though it was smaller than the water beast. The Obsidian's slim muzzle held rows of long and pointed teeth, and two giant curved horns sat on the back of its head. Every inch of the monster was covered in cracked, clinking and shrieking, scales of the black volcanic glass. The Lake Dragon spew large streams of boiling hot water at the Obsidian of Ruby, but it was useless. The hot water fell off the glass scales without leaving so much as a mark. It was like a warm shower to that wretched dragon.

On the other side, the Obsidian of Ruby's fierce flames also did very little to a dragon that constantly dove under the water to escape its burning intent.

Steam filled the air in hot bursts as the two of them battled, and Lady felt like the very air was cooking her and Nicholas in their armor.

The Lake Dragon, sensing the inevitable stalemate in distance attacks, made grabs for the circling black dragon. It used claws and teeth both to try and grab Obsidian of Ruby down into the water by his wings. The black dragon was too fast, however, and easily evaded every attack with quick twists and turns in the air. The Obsidian of Ruby made no move to grab at the Lake Dragon, however, and instead flew higher over its head.

"What is he doing?" Nicholas asked, steadying Martha to keep her from flying away too fast and missing the fight. "Why doesn't he attack?"

"That monster made of glass so he doesn't want to risk taking a hit," Lady whispered, terrified of drawing his attention. The target of all her rage and hate was right there, just waiting to be attacked by surprise but Lady couldn't move. She felt like a small child running through bodies in a terrified mob again. She held the burned side of her cheek, the area aching with a long past hurt. "And it is about to attack. Just watch."

The Obsidian of Ruby roared, flapping its wings back and forth hard. It shook his head and neck, sending a tremor down his entire spine. The glass cracked loudly, the shrieks of it filling the air. The dragon dove, and whipped its body hard to the side as it passed across the Lake Dragon, covering it in a sea of sharp glass. The Lake Dragon screamed as the shards stuck in between the shells and barnacles covering its body, though she imagined the ones that stuck into its eyes were far more painful.

The Lake Dragon hunched over, clawing at its own eyes in order to free the glass from its face. It was so distracted by the glass, that it didn't have time to move when the Obsidian of Ruby landed on the barnacle covered back and dug sharp claws into the joints of its wings.

Martha turned away at the sound of the rip, and the yank of the wing from the Lake Dragon's back. Lady kept her eyes locked on the scene, watching as the brutal attack occurred. The Obsidian of Ruby, now that it had found a hold, was unstoppable. It ripped the wings free from the other dragon, and dove its head straight into the wound. It came back with a mouthful of flesh, and the Lake Dragon made such a wailing, agonizing cry that Lady paled in fear.

The Lake Dragon collapsed in the marsh, twitching as the Obsidian of Ruby continued to eat it alive, diving its head further and further into the back of its flesh as it moaned in the water. Lady turned away, her stomach churning as she listened to the sound of bones and scales crunching.

It had all happened so fast, there had barely been a fight at all.

"We need to leave," Nicholas hissed. He grabbed Lady's shoulder and shook her to get her attention. "Now, before he sees us and decides he wants dessert."

Lady nodded, unable to speak and covered her mouth.

Nicholas turned them around, just as the Obsidian of Ruby roared into the night's sky, and dove down into the dark pit to ravage and destroy his kill's lair.

Lady threw up when she got back to her room.

Scrambling up the stairs and locking herself inside, she had dove for the small bucket in the corner. Lady clutched the edge of the bucket to keep her hands from shaking, the pressure of it threatening to crack the wood. Her stomach twisted and refused to cooperate as her mind tried to process what had happened. How could the Obsidian of Ruby be here? Her gut lurched. Why wasn't that monster back at home where it belonged? Lady coughed, trying to clear her throat of the acid. What were the odds of it attacking her kill?

Why was it here?

She emptied the last of the vile substance into the bowl, breathing heavily through the last of the dry heaves. Finally sure there was nothing else, Lady stood and wiped her mouth off with a towel. Her nerves had yet to completely settle, but there was something far more important she needed to check right now than her own shaking hands.

Lady ran across the hall and burst into Amadeus' room without so much as a knock. She scanned the area for him, nearly sobbing in relief when she found Amadeus napping in the side chair next to a desk.

She tugged him up into a smothering hug, neither caring that he was asleep nor without his armor. He grunted, his face buried in her shoulder and Lady squeezed him hard in response.

"Lady?" He mumbled, pushing to reposition himself into a more comfortable hold. "What's going on?"

"I'm so glad you listened and stayed here," Lady said, holding him tighter. Her fingers dug into his skin through the silk shirt, and she relished the heat of him. Lady knew she was being foolish. Amadeus had been in no danger. But all the same, Lady held him closer. "So, so glad."

Amadeus slowly shifted his hold to hug her back. He rubbed her side, slipping his fingers through the gaps in the armor to touch her side. He breathed softly, and Lady clung to the soothing sound. "What happened?"

"It showed up," Lady said, clutching to his shirt. She buried her face in his shoulder, desperately trying to block out the sight of that wretched dragon from her memories. "To attack the Lake Dragon. It was there and awful as ever."

"What was there?" Amadeus asked, pulling back enough to lift and cup her face. He brushed the side of her eye, wiping away the first hint of a worried tear. "Tell me what happened."

"The Obsidian of Ruby appeared to attack the Lake Dragon," Lady whispered. She grabbed Amadeus' shirt at his waist. Lady felt the hysteria sneaking into her very being and she hated it. She twisted the silk fabric beneath her gloves, begging for answers. "Why was it here? That monster is supposed to be at the Ruby Mines!"

"I think you of all people should know that he likes to travel around," Amadeus said, softly. He let go of her face and wrapped his arms around her waist in a loose hug. She accepted it, and concentrated on his voice. "The Southern Falls are no where near the Ruby Mines, are they?"

"No, they're not," Lady said, sucking in a shaky breath. She laughed, a nervous and sad sound even to her own ears. "But what are the odds?"

"Are you alright?" Amadeus asked, brushing her hair behind her ear. His thumb lingered on her cheek, warm and welcome.

"I thought I was ready for this," Lady said, her voice caught in her throat. She pressed her forehead into Amadeus' chest and grit her teeth. She had been so sure, and talked so big. And everything came crashing down in one, horrific moment. Lady buried herself in Amadeus, pressing harder into him. "I thought I was ready to fight him, I was so sure. But all it took was a single look and I froze. It was as if time had reversed and all my training and preparation had meant nothing. I couldn't do it. I could barely move."

"You haven't seen him since you were little, have you?" Amadeus asked, rubbing her back up and down.

"No," Lady whispered. She tugged and pulled Amadeus closer, burying her face in his shirt. "I hate that monster so much."

Amadeus continued to hug her, long until the morning light.

Lady sat on her bed, her face covered with both of her hands. Amadeus had stepped out to fetch some bread and soup for lunch, and she was officially sulking. Her terror and panic had faded away enough that Lady could think clearly again, and that was when the embarrassment had taken the panic's place. Lady dug her fingers into her hair, thinking of the night with Amadeus.

Of all her little day dreams of sharing a bed with him, last night had never been a part of it.

She'd clutched and coddled up to him like a little girl wanting her father to hold her after a nightmare. And he'd done it! Amadeus held her, cooing and rubbing her back as Lady cried on him all night. Lady was a dragon slayer. A fierce warrior! How could she be reduced to such pathetic, childish tears with just one look at the Obsidian of Ruby in battle?

When did it all get so out of control?

"So embarrassing," Lady groaned into her hands. She rolled onto her side and huffed into the pillow. How was she ever going to face Amadeus again after that? "What must he think of me?"

"Ah, Lady," Nicholas said, poking his head into the room. Lady yanked the pillow down and glared at the intruding man. Couldn't he see she was pouting? Nicholas rubbed the back of his neck, and smiled sheepishly. "I hate to interrupt, but do you have a dress that Martha could borrow?"

"Martha?" Lady rolled over and sat up. She leaned on her bent legs, and scratched at her loose hair. "What on earth would she need a dress for?"

"Because he insists that running around naked is too much for his delicate eyes," Martha said, poking her human head through the door under his arm. She had a cape wrapped around her, and bare feet stuck out from the bottom. Unlike before, her transformation had more time to settle, leaving her indistinguishable from any other human. Martha's red hair fell flat, long and straight, and her skin was still dark, though now free of leftover scales. "So if you wouldn't mind, I'd like to borrow something so I don't have to hear him whine about it."

"Martha," Nicholas hissed. "Be nice."

"I will not," Martha growled right back. She shoved him in the side, and kicked his shin. Nicholas flinched at both hits, holding his hands up like she'd whack him again. "It's bad enough I have to stay like this, so don't you even start with that."

"Why is she in human form?" Lady asked, getting out of the bed. Perhaps this distraction was exactly what she needed. Nicholas and Martha shenanigans did wonders for drawing all attention in the room to them. Lady pulled over her bag, and rustled around inside for a spare shirt and pants.

"Because I will not be a target!" Martha said. She waved her hand at the window toward the marsh. "Dragons attract dragons and I have no idea if that beast Obsidian is still around, or if his sudden appearance has brought other dragons coming to look for him. I'm not taking the risk."

"Martha feels it is safer to hide in town as a human, than to be out in the open as a dragon in the fields," Nicholas clarified. "And as such, she is in need of some clothes."

"Right," Lady said.

She threw an outfit at Martha and ducked under Nicholas' other arm to leave the room in almost a single motion. While the distraction had cleared her head, it had almost done too good of a job. Lady had too much to think about, and probably too much to do considering their spoiled plans, and none of it was going to get done if she sat there and listened to those two bickering.

Lady skipped down the stairs of the inn, passing the main lobby and heading out into the muddy streets. She walked down them, passing people gossiping and whispering at each other. The words "lake" and "obsidian" hung on their breaths, and it wasn't hard to imagine what had made the news that morning. There was no way that the Lake Dragon's body hadn't been found yet, and it was sure to be covered with Obsidian scales everywhere. It didn't take a genius to put together what had happened. Lady walked by them all, leaving them as an empty thought in her head as she made her way to the community center.

The back gate was open, and Lady let herself in to see the gardens in the daylight. The roses were still in bloom, and Lady breathed in the scent. It was calming in a way that nothing else could be. She walked down the path, her armor unnaturally loud in the quiet area, and sat down on the metal bench she had been on a couple nights before.

"I had a feeling you might show up here," Amadeus said, sitting a few feet to her left on top of the garden wall. He plucked the petals off of an orchid, tossing each one to the ground as he went. "I'm glad it was right, or I might have been out here alone all night."

"Why aren't you back at the inn?" Lady asked, pulling a foot up on the bench. "I thought you were out getting lunch for us."

"I had a hunch that you might not be there when I returned," Amadeus said. He hopped down from the wall, tossing the half plucked orchid over his shoulder. He joined Lady on the bench, and crossed his legs as he sat. "A change of scenery can be good when you need time to think."

Lady nodded, and scooted over to give him more room. He used that same space to scoot closer, so that their thighs touched, armor to armor.

"Have you thought about what you're going to do?" Amadeus asked. He touched her shoulder, drawing a small circle in the armor there with his gloves. "Are you still planning to go the Ruby Mines now that you've seen him in person again?"

"Yes," Lady said. She folded her hands in her lap, and leaned her head back to look at the blue sky above. A few birds flew by, but the sky was fairly empty. "I've made a decision concerning that."

Amadeus tapped her shoulder once, shifting ever so slightly on the bench. "And what would that be?"

"I still want to go," Lady said. She leaned forward, resting her elbows on her knees. She laced her fingers together, and touched her forehead to her hands. "I need to go."

"And what do you plan to accomplish by doing so?" Amadeus asked, touching a hand to her back. "Surely you've noticed the folly in trying to attack him?"

"It's not about that anymore," Lady said. She breathed heavily through her nose, in and out as steady as she could. Lady licked her lips. "I want to be able to see him. I want to see him, and not cower in fear. No, wanting isn't enough. I need this."

"Oh?" Amadeus asked. "And you'll do that by going to confront him?"

"Yes," Lady said. She looked up and over her shoulder. She locked eyes with Amadeus and sat up without breaking that contact. "I need to be able to stand in a room with him and not be afraid."

"Then as always," Amadeus said, brushing her hair out of her face. He leaned over and kissed her on the cheek, so close to the side of the mouth that it was almost a tease. "I wish you the best of luck with your endeavor."

Amadeus left Lady sitting alone in the garden to think. She touched the side of the cheek where his lips met, and she could have sworn it felt hot enough to burn. Lady kissed her fingertips and closed her eyes.

She needed to go there and put all this behind her.

Or Lady would never be able to move on.

Chapter 15

AS THE GIRL grew, however, she learned more and more things. And as humans often do, she grew curious about the world. What was beyond the valley? What would she see? Why did she live so much longer than her loving family of ruby roses?

These are the questions she asked herself and the ruby roses near daily. They had no answers for her, and the birds in the sky would only sing in response.

To find her answers, the young girl might very well have to leave the ones that gave her life. They loved each other so dearly. She knew they would always be a part of her, and she a part of them forever. They must know it, too.

So why did they sob so when she asked to leave the valley?

"I am afraid we must part ways now," Nicholas said, walking over to rest his hands on Lady and Amadeus' shoulders. He grinned, despite the regretful look in his eyes. Martha hovered behind him, back in her full dragon form, fidgeting and moving back and forth in her desperation to leave. "I would love to come with you the rest of the way, but Martha is most insistent that we both go home for now."

"And how could you tell that gorgeous face 'no', am I right?" Lady said. She slapped Nicholas on the arm, and followed it up with a light punch from her knuckles on his chest. "No hard feelings on this end, but you had better keep in touch."

"That I most certainly will make sure to do," Nicholas said, patting his side pocket. "I have yours, Amadeus', and Agatha's addresses all safe and sound in my pouch and plan to write very often."

"I look forward to those letters," Lady said. She gave Nicholas one last big hug, squeezing tight. She turned to Amadeus, and waved the pale man over. "Come on, another hug won't kill you. Give Nicholas a proper goodbye."

"If you insist," Amadeus said. He embraced Nicholas with a polite hug, and shook his hand afterwards. "Feel free to write at any time."

"I will," Nicholas said. He yanked Amadeus over and gave him a bear hug that lifted the proper man a foot off the ground before setting him back on his feet. "You can count on it."

Lady giggled, as Amadeus straightened his hair and his armor from the hug. Nicholas, too, chuckled and climbed up onto Martha's back. He waved as the two of them flew off into the sky. Nicholas called out a few las goodbyes as Martha flew high and fast.

"I'm going to miss him," Lady said, leaning her head toward Amadeus. She held a hand up to block the sun, and watched Martha's ruby scales glitter in the sun as they flew off. "He's so full of life, I'm jealous."

"I think it's his dragon that was jealous," Amadeus said. He climbed into the carriage, and shoved over a bag to sit down in his usual place. "She didn't care for us much, did she?"

"I rather say she didn't care for Nicholas, either," Lady said. She plopped down across from Amadeus and sprawled out on the seat. She waved at Drake as he shut the carriage door behind. Lady hummed, stretching her arms out over her head. "Though she did get rather protective of him when we went after the Lake Dragon, so maybe I was wrong."

"She is very fond of him," Amadeus said, with a knowing look. "It's very easy to tell when you can look past the dragon part of her."

"You're saying my immediate hatred of her clouded my judgement?" Lady snorted.

"That's exactly what I am saying," Amadeus said. He pulled out the box of wine, and signaled for Drake to get the carriage moving before he attempted to pour a cup. "Speaking, are you absolutely sure about what you're doing?"

"This time, I am," Lady said. She covered her eyes and shifted in the seat. "I need to know I can at least face him without falling apart like I did before. Then, then maybe I can really prepare."

"You still aim to kill him then?" Amadeus asked.

Lady put her hands down, and turned her head to the side to face him. The words felt as natural as breathing as she said, "I do."

With no more distractions in their way, the final leg to the Ruby Mines was a rather quick trip. They stopped in three towns on the way, spending a night or two in each inn and taking in the sights. Amadeus had filled his carriage with sweets and tourist traps from each city, and Lady allowed herself to relax for a few moments here or there in his company.

Amadeus did his best to keep Lady's mind occupied on other things, but the knot in her gut grew larger and larger the closer they came to the Ruby Mines. The monstrous mountainside that hid her worst nightmare had come into view in the far distance, and there was no denying that she was close to seeing that dragon again. Lady sat up against the window of the carriage, having pulled it open for the first time. She ignored the mountains and watched the countryside pass by, the green grasses and the tall trees running for miles.

Amadeus scooted across the carriage and sat next to her, leaning forward toward the window. He pointed to a spot over the nearest hill. "That's the last town before we arrive at my home."

"Which town is it?" Lady asked, leaning back so that they touched.

"Strawberry Lake," Amadeus said. He tugged lightly on a wave of her hair, and sat back against the seat. "Famous for strawberries as big and as red as our largest rubies."

"Sounds delicious," Lady said. She moved away from the window, and rested against his side. "I'm sure that'll be a wonderful treat."

"Would you mind if I kissed you?" Amadeus asked, oddly serious and out of the blue.

Lady froze, staring at the cushion in front of her. "What brought that up?"

"You mentioned a treat, and it finally hit me that we are alone, and have no where else we need to be," Amadeus said. He pulled off his glove, and touched Lady's cheek with his fingers. He pulled her head to face him, delicately and as gently as he had inspected that ruby when they first met. "And I thought to myself it was something I would very much like to do."

"Only just now?" Lady asked, turned enough in the seat that she drew one knee up into it. Amadeus had always been a tease, with light pecks to the side of her cheek or her knuckles, but never this straight forward. Lady rather liked it, and so did her heart as it picked up a beat. She placed a hand on his thigh, and pressed into it as she pushed up closer to his face. "It just popped into your head?"

"Only that this was a good opportunity," Amadeus leaned in, "to do what I've been thinking about since you first stole a piece of sausage off my plate."

Lady kissed him, hard and firm on his lips. The man with the wonderful laugh, and wonderful green eyes had let Lady cry in his lap for hours and still wanted to kiss her. *How dare he be so handsome*, she thought in a rush of want. She grabbed the back of his head and crawled into the seat to sit up higher. Wrapping her arms around his shoulders, Lady opened her mouth to kiss him again and again until he did the same. His tongue burned against hers, everything about him was heat and warmth once you got past his icy demeanor. It was a glorious contradiction of his person, and she wanted to drink all of it down.

Lady couldn't get enough of it.

She broke the kiss to catch her breath, half in his lap, and half on the cushion. She clutched at the back of his head, and pressed their faces together, pecking his cheek. Lady asked, "Should I have asked first?"

"No," Amadeus answered, his voice hoarse. His hands clutched at her hips, and she breathed heavily. "I don't mind at all."

"Then for the record," Lady said, "You may kiss me all you want."

Amadeus greedily accepted Lady's permission and kissed her long and deeply, with little breaks for air as he shoved her down into the seat cushion. With his hips against hers, the mountains seemed farther away than ever.

Lady hardly had any complaints.

Strawberry Lake had been as lovely as Amadeus had hinted when mentioning their namesake, but it wasn't the lovely walk and strawberry cakes during the day that had her stomach in flutters. It was the night.

Lady stood at the end of Amadeus' bed, holding the top edge of her nightgown in her hand. She twisted the fabric around her fingers, the room dark save for the sliver of moonlight spilling out onto the floor. Lady walked to the side of the bed, and sat on the edge. Amadeus rested peacefully, his face relaxed and breath even. This was it. This was the time.

Lady had time for this, the Obsidian of Ruby be damned.

She'd thought about it on and off since that first drunken night at the bar. Teased about it, and even made little plans for a one night here or there, but Lady wanted this. After that moment in the carriage Lady couldn't wait any longer. She had permission. She was wanted, and the Obsidian of Ruby wasn't going to die any time soon. Amadeus, though, may be gone forever after this trip ended. There was no guarantee she'd see him again after they reached the Ruby Mines and he went back to his First Family and riches. If she wanted this, she would have to do it now.

Lady reached down, and brushed his hair aside. She rubbed his shoulder, and whispered, "Amadeus."

He awoke with a slight jerk, and green eyes focused on Lady. He glanced around the room, and looked back up at her face. "Is something the matter?"

"Nothing," Lady said, wincing slightly. The last time she had woken him up like this, she'd sobbed in his arms. Perhaps Lady should have considered sneaking in when he was getting ready for bed instead of when he had already gone to sleep. Lady waved her hand back and forth. "Nothing's wrong."

"Did you need something?" He asked, shifting and keeping his focus on Lady.

She slipped off the bed, and pulled the covers back. He sat up exposed, his nightshirt hanging loosely on his thin frame. *Now or never, Lady*, she told herself. Lady pulled her nightgown over her head, revealing her chest. The full extents of her burns were open to the air, covering nearly all of her shoulder and half of her breasts. His eyes widened, and he swallowed, shifting on the mattress. She dropped her nightgown and slipped back onto the bed, sliding under the covers before he could say anything.

Lady hugged him around the shoulders and drew in close. His breath hitched in just the right way that made her heart skip so delightfully, and she whispered, "I was hoping you'd like some company."

Amadeus kissed her mouth, tender and sweet.

Lady tugged him over, and rested his hand on her side. Without the armor between them, she was able to feel every inch of his lean muscle and burning skin. She kissed him back, and dug her fingers into his slick

136

hair. He kissed her once more on the shoulder, and settled there. Amadeus hugged her tightly, his face on half of her breast, and his arms wrapped around her. Lady pressed his face firmly into her chest, and rolled her hips a bit, but he didn't move.

"Amadeus?" She asked, her heart pounding under her ribs.

What if he doesn't want it?

"As much as I would adore to make love to you," he whispered into her breast, his breath warmer than an oven. Lady's breath hitched as he squeezed her side and nuzzled her skin. "I would very much like to wait, until after you see my home."

"May I ask why?" Lady asked, holding him tighter to her chest. "Is a few days and a house really going to make so much of a difference?"

"I want to make sure you won't change your mind about me after you see it," Amadeus said. He pulled the blankets tight around them, and closed his eyes. He kissed her breast and sighed into her skin. "Is that so much to ask for?"

"No," she whispered. Lady petted his hair, and rested her head against his pillow. She held him against her, and closed her own eyes. He was warm, and his skin felt so right against hers. Lady wanted him to hold her forever. How could she risk this? "I can wait."

"Thank you," he said. He squeezed her tightly around the waist, and nuzzled his nose into her breast. "But I wouldn't mind if you stayed with me tonight, just like this."

Lady relaxed against him, closing her eyes and breathing in the scent of him. "Neither would I."

Chapter 16

AGAINST THE WISHES of the ruby roses, the girl left her home in the valley. Dressed in the feathers that had fallen from birds and leaves she had gathered from the mountainside trees, the girl walked and walked until she had left the small valley behind. The girl had every intention of returning, but only after she had seen more of the world. Why was that so hard for her family to understand?

It took her a few days, but she finally found more people along the road to a small village. They stared at her and her clothing, and she grew uncomfortable comparing her own dressings to those around her. She rose above it, though, knowing full well she was a child of the esteemed ruby roses.

People also called her an odd thing as she passed, not knowing what it meant, she assumed that it must have been her name. That was something that was given, was it not? And her loving family had not given her one yet, so that must have been it.

When they asked where she was from, she said 'The Roses', and they started to change her name accordingly.

The Ruby Mines were every bit the extravagant countrysides that they had become known for. Rich fields covered in flowers surrounded the towns and villages that were dotted around the mines. All of them beautiful and well kept from the poorest house to the richest mansion. Of the area, the two biggest landmarks were the Capitol City and the volcano that was home to the Obsidian of Ruby that conveniently sat side by side.

The mountainous volcano loomed over them in the distance as

Amadeus' carriage drove down the main street of the Capitol City. Lady scowled at it, and sat back in her seat, shutting the window firmly. "You said we're staying at your place?"

"Yes," Amadeus said, sorting out a few papers on his lap. He folded them neatly and shoved them into a large envelop before replacing it in his bag. "At the castle."

"The castle, huh?" Lady asked. She packed up her loose things into her bag and smirked. "I don't know why that information refuses to sink in, despite all I've seen of you. Hard to believe a down to earth guy like you is living with royalty."

"Ha ha, I believe is the proper response," Amadeus said. He straightened out his belongings, before turning to his armor and cloak. Amadeus pulled out a small vanity mirror and checked his hair and face in a distracted manor. "But you'll see for yourself soon enough."

As soon as the carriage pulled to a stop at the front gate of the castle, the door was whisked open by a man servant who was not Drake. Another two servants rushed passed Lady and headed for their trunk. A butler dressed in finery that put most of Lady's wardrobe to shame, greeted them warmly as servant upon servant took their bags and belongs out of the carriage and into the castle doors.

Drake stepped down from the driver's seat of the carriage, running a hand through his blond hair to straighten it out. The man fixed his suit and ruby broach before taking a spot next to the head butler. Lady bit her lip when the older man adjusted Drake's neck tie before scolding him. It was funny to think Amadeus wasn't the only one who got to order that poor man around. Drake was forgotten however, as Amadeus stepped out of the carriage.

"Master Amadeus," the butler greeted, bowing deeply at the waist. "We're so happy that you made it back safely. We received all of your letters, and rooms have been cleaned and prepared as requested for your two guests."

"It'll only be one, I'm afraid," Amadeus said, stepping down from the carriage. Lady waited for him to mention a name of some sort, but it didn't seem to be coming. Amadeus fixed his gloves and adjusted his cloak, his shoulders straight and back in a commanding fashion. "My second guest had to cancel his stay at the last minute."

"Dreadfully sorry to hear, sir," the butler said. He turned to Lady and nodded, "Ma'am, it is a pleasure to have you staying with us."

"Uh, sure," Lady said, glancing around at all the well dressed people. She shifted, rubbing the side of her dented armor and felt oddly out of place. It was a rare feeling for Lady and she wanted it to go away as soon as possible Lady nodded at the butler and trotted to catch up with Amadeus as he strode toward the front doors with Drake in tow. Realizing a second later Lady left without saying anything, she turned and shouted back at him, "Glad to be here!"

Amadeus chuckled at her, and she hit him in the side. Lady waved over her shoulder at the ten or so people still unpacking the carriage and standing at attention down the line. "Well that's quite the welcome, isn't it?"

"Anything less would be considered an insult for someone of my standing," Amadeus said. He waved his finger back and forth. "You know everything about dragons, but you really must learn some social etiquette."

"Etiquette in the Ruby Mines isn't the same as in the Southern Falls and you know it," Lady said. Drake coughed to cover up a laugh of his own, and Lady rolled her eyes at the quiet man. Amadeus was smiling too, though, so it wasn't all too bad to have a laugh at her expense every now and again. Lady held her arms behind her back and leaned her head back to stare at the ceiling soaring high above her head. "But still, this place is huge."

Amadeus deadpanned, "It's a castle."

"You know what I meant!" Lady said, shoving him on the side again. The force of it nearly knocked him over and he stumbled for a few steps before correcting himself and cleaning off the side of his armor with his traveling cape like nothing had happened. She laughed at the aghast look that the servants sent their direction from the casual banter. Feeling mischievous, she decided they could use more to gossip about anyway. Lady took Amadeus by the elbow and leaned on his arm. "So where to first, Mr. Noble?"

"First," Amadeus said, turning down a hallway. He patted Lady's arm that held his, and with a bitter smile said, "I must stop and greet mother."

"Mother?" Lady stopped dead in the hallway.

Amadeus' mother was an old woman with shaking hands and fierce, familiar green eyes. Not a single white hair piled on top of her head was out of place. The tight bun had been twisted so tightly it made Lady's own head ache looking at it. Everything about her was tension and anger, and even her wrinkles looked strained. Lady waited at the doorway, unsure if she was welcome during this visit as Amadeus passed by her. The air was thick, like a room full of steam. Lady felt like there was an invisible wall preventing her from passing the threshold. Lady stepped inside only when Amadeus asked for the door to be closed.

"It's good to see you well," Amadeus said to his mother. He kissed her on the forehead, his fingers gently brushing the side of her face, before walking past her to the vanity and mirror along the wall. His voice was light, but there was something hidden in it that set Lady's nerves on end. Amadeus added, "I have missed you."

His mother neither moved, nor turned her head. She did nothing to acknowledge that Amadeus had entered the room or had spoken to her. Lady drew her arms up to hug herself, as she walked a few steps farther inside to see what he was doing at the vanity pressed against the far wall. There was something unspeakably cold in this room, and it sent chills down her spine.

Amadeus opened a polished wooden jewelry box, and pulled out a small pin with a delicate ruby stone embedded in a metal flower. He brushed his gloved finger over the surface, freeing it from imaginary dust. Lady watched quietly as he returned to his mother, and reached around to pull off a pin attached to the front of her blouse. Amadeus switched the old pin for the new one, and set the old one back into the jewelry box. He closed the lid with a click, frowning heavily.

Lady shifted, unsure of why he was so upset.

"They never change her pin out when they dress her," Amadeus explained, picking up on the unspoken question. He patted the top of the jewelry box, leaning his hip against the side of the vanity. "She has so many lovely things to wear, and yet they never bother to let her do so. I really must have a word with them about it."

"I see," Lady said, swallowing. Amadeus' mother had still yet to move, aside from the constant trembling of her hands and arms. She could have sworn she saw awareness in the old woman's eyes, but the frozen behavior led to doubts. Perhaps she wasn't all there in the head any longer. Lady leaned toward Amadeus and whispered, "Is she alright?"

"Mother?" Amadeus laughed. It was a cruel sound, so unlike the other amused laughter Lady had grown to adore. It was bitter. Mocking.

Amadeus brushed Lady's hair behind her ear, his finger lingering near the side of her cheek. The warm touch was distracting, and perhaps he meant it to be as Lady found herself staring hard at the woman in the chair. "She's fine. Mother is merely angry with me."

"What's she angry about?" Lady asked, attempting to keep her voice down. The woman didn't look at them, and she wondered if the old woman could still hear. "To be so still and to ignore you that way?"

"A long time ago I stole something very precious from her," Amadeus said, walking closer to his mother. He put his hands on her shoulders from the back, and kissed the side of her head again. Amadeus squeezed the elder woman's shoulders. "And she has never forgiven me.

"No one holds a grudge like a mother," Amadeus said. He stroked the back of her chair with the edge of his fingertip, and headed back for the hall door.

Lady crossed the room, pausing by the old woman's chair. The question left her lips before she could stop it. "What did you take?"

Amadeus shook his head and walked into the hallway, "It's nothing important any longer."

He had lied.

Lady hugged herself even harder, and looked at the ground. Amadeus never lied to her. Lady considered herself a good judge of character when it came to those things. What could he have taken that he needed to lie about it after all these years? That his mother could still be so furious about? Lady dropped her arms. She rubbed the back of her neck, her fingers digging into the skin. Is this what he was talking about in the hotel when he said he wanted to wait until Lady knew more? As she moved to leave, the old woman grabbed her wrist.

Lady yelped, turning to look down at the wrinkled hand that squeezed her armor as tightly as it could. The old woman opened her mouth as if she was going to say something, but then closed it with a snap. Lady could hear her teeth grinding in her old mouth as she hissed. Amadeus' mother let go of Lady's arm and fell back in her chair. She sighed heavily and sunk into the backing like the world had fallen on her chest.

"Ma'am?" Lady asked.

"Go," she whispered. "Just go."

Lady left the room, and found Amadeus watching her in the hallway.

He closed the door for her, and carefully watched Lady's face. "Did she say something?"

"I think she wanted to," Lady said, "but no, she didn't."

Amadeus nodded, and took her arm by the elbow. "Come on then, I'll show you where your room is."

Lady's room was larger than most inn suites. She had a full sitting room, a bedroom, and a sprawling balcony all to herself in this corner of the castle. If this is how a guest of a First Family Noble was treated, Lady was almost terrified to think of where she might be staying had she been a guest of the King instead. Lady saw her belongings already moved to the room. She tired to ignore how tiny and insignificant her bag looked placed next to the king-sized poster bed.

"I had the butler remove any and all doilies that might have been in here," Amadeus said, leaning against the door Lady walked around the room. "So hopefully it's to your liking?"

"It's perfect," Lady said. She threw open the balcony doors, and walked out onto the high terrace. Lady leaned on the railing and breathed in the calm night air. She could still feel his mother's hand on her arm, even through the armor. She rubbed her face and focused on the matter at hand. "You'd think that the air here would be less clean with so many mines about."

"We're very careful about what equipment we use to excavate," Amadeus said, joining her on the balcony. His cape swayed softy in the breeze, making him look more regal than before. Amadeus waved below them at a field of grass and flowers. "Wouldn't want to upset the local wildlife too much."

Lady followed the field of flowers until they reached the horizon line. The mountain of a volcano was hard to miss so close to the town. Lady grabbed the banister tightly. "When's a good time to go see it?"

"We could go exploring his hoard now, if you wanted," Amadeus said. He leaned against the railing and watched Lady instead of the mountain. He crossed his arm on the banister and laughed. "It's not too far of a trip by horse back."

"Now?" Lady asked. Part of her was in just that sort of rush, but the hour was also late. Surely Drake or some other servant would have an issue with the two of them sneaking out to see the dragon, wouldn't they? She waved at the far off volcano and rolled a finger around in the air. "Wouldn't it be better to go during the day while he's asleep?"

"It doesn't matter much if it's day or night when he's not in there," Amadeus said. He rubbed the bottom of his chin and licked the side of his lip. "Though now that I think about it, a morning trip might be better."

"How do you know he isn't there?" Lady asked. She ignored the twisting nausea in her stomach that she had come all this way just to wait again. "Shouldn't it have come straight here after stealing the hoard from the Lake Dragon?"

"He could still have it on him. Dragons do tend to carry things around in their Hoard Guts until it's full," Amadeus said, shrugging and pushing himself off the railing. He smoothed his hair back with both hands. "The Obsidian of Ruby is rather picky about what goes into his hoard, so I doubt he took everything. Only the finest."

Lady rubbed her thumb against the side of her armor. "And the first question?"

"There's no smoke," Amadeus said. He pointed to the mountain, and drew a small circle around an area near the base. "Our obsidian scaled friend has a rather large bonfire in there, and when he's home, he lights it. No one is stupid enough to steal from him, but he does like to let everyone in the surrounding villages know when he's there so they'll keep quiet."

"How considerate," Lady said. The power of Great Dragons was surreal some days. Had they so little fear that they announced their presence so honestly? Lady rubbed her face, and turned away from the mountain. "Why is the morning trip better than going right now?"

"I'm delivering his tribute tomorrow morning, so you might as well accompany me at the drop off. You can get a good feel for his home," Amadeus said. He leaned in close, whispering in her ear, "So that when he's in it later and you decide to pay a visit, you'll know where you need to run."

Lady nodded, having no answer for the second part of that statement. "Morning it is."

"Until then," Amadeus said, kissing the side of her cheek. His lips waited there, as if asking silent permission to continue. Lady leaned ever so slightly away to break the contact, her fingers wringing together at her waist. Amadeus didn't seem bothered, his eyes as warm as ever as he smiled and left with a soft set of parting words. "Have sweet dreams and a good night."

Lady wasn't sure what kept her from asking him to stay for a few hours more, but the cold feeling in her stomach continued to grow the longer she stayed foot in this castle.

The morning couldn't come soon enough.

"You call this a gemstone!" Amadeus shouted, throwing the rock across the room. The cowering assistant ducked, trembling as the other man berated him. Lady stayed against the wall, her mouth and eyes agape. Drake yawned into his hand next to her, bored and shoulders dropped. As if he'd seen this display a thousand times before. Lady glanced at him and back to the screaming Amadeus trying to process this information:

This was normal behavior for him.

She'd traveled with the man for close to a month now and had never seen such a temper come from the calm and collected man. Even when he'd been furious at being left behind with the Sandstone dragon, his anger had been quiet and controlled. He'd dressed up to look superior to her and gave Lady the silent treatment. Lady flinched as Amadeus tossed an entire box of rubies onto the floor in an angry sweep across the desk. This was violence.

Lady bit her tongue. *Where had he been hiding this?*

"For a second hand pawn shop they might pass, but these are for the Obsidian of Ruby! It's an insult!" Amadeus yelled, shoving the stones across the floor back at the other men with the side of his foot. "I clearly can not trust any of you to handle this in my absence, can I?"

"We-we're so sorry sir," A man groveled. He held his hands up between himself and Amadeus, low to the ground and bowing his head. "We did our best, but you weren't here to help with the final quality control, and it's the best that we had and—"

"Do better," Amadeus hissed.

Lady crossed her arms and stared at the floor. Perhaps it was the location. He was on his best behavior running around in foreign cities and towns, but was himself at home. Maybe this was it, and not his strained relationship with his mother that had Amadeus warning Lady about relations with him.

He had said he wanted Lady to see his home, but she believed now he should have phrased it better. As Amadeus continued to yell, and Drake continued to look bored by the display, Lady wondered if she was grateful or not at having been a warning. She watched his eyes light up in ferocity, and his handsome face contort in anger and wondered if it mattered if this is what he was really like.

Part of Lady didn't care, still clinging to the warm laugh and passionate kisses in his carriage or the gentle kiss to her cheek last night.

His tantrum ended a few moments later, Amadeus breathing heavily and his hair fallen out of place. He fixed it with a swipe of his hand and a final glare at the other men in the room.

"I hope that I have made myself clear," Amadeus said. He pulled over a box from the other side of the table and sorted through them with a wave of his hand. He plucked five from the box and threw them into a small velvet sack. "The Obsidian of Ruby might take this pitiful offering this time, if we're lucky. But unless you want him burning down the entire countryside, I suggest you find him something nicer for the next trip."

"Yes, sir!" They cried in unison.

"Now clean this up!" Amadeus said, flicking his hand at the lot of them and the mess Amadeus himself had made.

They scrambled to gather up the fallen gemstones, shoving them back into the small case they had come in. Amadeus flicked his cape back over his shoulder and proceeded to ignore them.

Lady clutched her arms to herself and once again realized just how little she knew about this man.

"Idiots," he mumbled next to Lady. She swallowed, and he dropped his angry expression in a heartbeat upon seeing her face. Amadeus held the bag up for Lady to take, and she held it gently. Amadeus touched her face, and softened his expression. "I'm sorry you had to see that, but I expect only the very best from these men, and to deliver anything less is shameful."

"For a dragon who terrorizes the area," Lady said, clutching the bag to her chest. "You sure do your best to please it."

"It's part of the deal we have," Amadeus said. He opened the door for her into the lavish grand hallway in the East Wing of the castle. Their boots clicked on the smooth tiles as they walked, Amadeus and Lady in front with Drake trailing behind like the shadow he was. Every servant stopped and bowed as Amadeus passed, and Lady clutched the bag of gems harder. "They provide the best of the best of their take from the mines, and in exchange their home remains intact and not burnt to a crisp.

"I have to be harsh because what is given must be the best. If they get to comfortable, or forget just what they're dealing with, it could mean disaster. So I must be cruel," Amadeus continued, opening the door for them to leave. "Or else everyone will suffer for it."

Lady nodded quietly and followed him out the door.

Chapter 17

THE GIRL SPENT her days learning and loving everyone that she came to greet. The roses had taught her to enjoy and to love all, adoring and praising with her every breath. As such, she was most welcome no matter where she went.

The strangers would always call her by the same odd name when talking about her, so she would always helpfully interject, "Of the Roses" for them. The name soon became so well known that by the time she reached the next town, they were already calling her by her proper title.

She loved it all so, but alas, she missed her home. The girl traveled for miles and miles until she at last arrived back in her valley with her ruby roses. Never before had there been such a cry of welcome from the roses and wild life when she arrived.

"I have good news," she said. The girl opened up her arms wide. "I have a name now!"

"What name? What name?" they cried on the wind.

"I am Lady of the Roses," She said, "and I am so happy to be home."

And for the rest of her days, she stayed with the roses and they were happy.

The ride out to the dragon's lair was not far on horseback, as Amadeus had said. Lady supposed they could have made it out faster, but there seemed to be no rush. The ride was smooth and easy across the relatively flat area that sat between the City and the base of the mountain, and she was glad that it was only the two of them making the ride out there. It gave Lady time to clear her head, and to think about all the new things she was learning about Amadeus from only a day and a half at his home.

Estranged mother, dedication to his people by serving a beast to the best of his ability, a violent streak. If she had learned this much in such a short time, who knows what she'd have learned about him after a week or a month?

A small voice in the back of her head reminded Lady that she'd asked for this. Ever since they shared a dance, she'd wanted to know more.

Lady watched the side of his head as they rode along on their way, and felt her heartbeat pick up. This man never failed to send her insides for a loop, in every way possible. Lady twisted her hands around the reins of her borrowed horse, and picked up the pace.

She had a lifetime to get to know Amadeus, but she could only start once this other matter had been taken care of first. That was the plan. It had always been the plan.

The dormant volcano was a towering monster, shooting up in the sky for miles in rocky crags and spires. The terrain was uneven, and unwelcome to their steeds. Lady felt her boots hit the rocks of the ground, and sucked in a warm breath in the heavy air. They tied the horses to a nearby tree, and Amadeus took the lead on foot. He strode easily up a twisting path that only he could see through the rocks and natural obstacles in the side of the mountain, slowing his pace only to let Lady follow more closely.

"You sure know your way around up here," Lady said, stepping over a sizable rock. Amadeus turned another corner, his answer only a knowing smile. Lady huffed, and hurried to keep up before she got lost in the fallen rocks that surrounded the cave entrance.

Amadeus laughed a moment later, and admitted "I'm up here quite a bit."

"Dropping things off?" Lady asked. She hopped down after him when they reached a small dip in their path. Just beyond it, was a large opening that was big enough to fit a cathedral through it. A gaping hole in the side of the mountain that Lady probably could have seen from her room in the castle had she known to look for it. The cave beyond it was pitch black, and she heard the wind whistling through it. "Isn't it a bit odd for someone of your rank to be doing such a menial task?"

"I wouldn't think so," Amadeus said. He waved her forward and held out his hand for her as they entered the dark. "This way."

She took his hand and let him lead her through the threshold and into the large tunnel. The air was hot and dry, and full of thick black ash that made it hard to breathe. Lady had been told the volcano was no longer active, and had only erupted once in its lifetime, but she wondered how anyone could trust such information with all this heat around them. Something more than a dragon slept in this cave, and it was only time before it made itself known. Lady held tight to Amadeus' hand, and squeezed when they stopped.

The walk seemed to go on forever as they trailed along in the dark, but Amadeus never wavered nor slowed. He knew exactly where he was going. The confidence radiated off him, and Lady found it as comforting as she did unnerving. After remember her last encounter with the Obsidian of Ruby, and the memory of her body trembling in fear, she wondered if she could steal some of that bravery this man had from years of familiarity.

"Stay right here for just a moment," Amadeus said. He let go of her hand, leaving her side. "I'll be just a moment."

Lady stood alone in the dark, listening to Amadeus' footsteps as he crossed the room. The pounding of his boots was disturbed every so often by soft clinks, and the music of shifting metal. Coins, perhaps? Lady held the small bag of rubies in her hand, turning the gemstones around through the fabric of the sack. Lady bit the edge of her lip as she focused on Amadeus' footsteps on the stone flooring, reminding herself that she was not alone in here.

There was a crack and a hiss off to the side before a large light burst into the room. To her left, a giant fire roared, eating away at giant logs arranged into a bonfire pit. The fire licked the ceiling and thick clouds of smoke poured out through a small opening. Amadeus lit a torch from the blaze and pulled it to the side wall. He dipped it into a trough dug into the wall, and a fire lit, running all around the room in the slim pathway.

Lady gasped, as the darkness melted away, revealing giant mountains of golden coins and gemstones as far as the eye could see. Jewelry, raw chunks of ore, giant carved statues, and everything glittery, golden and silver was poured out and stuffed into every rock, nook and cranny of the giant room. The stacks of treasure towered high up until they touched the ceilings. Lady took a few steps back just to take everything in.

This was a true dragon's hoard.

"If you wouldn't mind?" Amadeus asked, holding his hand out.

Lady passed over the bag of rubies, eyes still trying to take in even a fraction of the treasure hoard that surrounded her, and Amadeus spilled them out into his hand. He arranged them neatly between the golden coins in a stack off to the side. Lady ignored him, her eyes locked on a small pile of treasure to her front. She walked toward it, drawn by an unknown force, putting her back to Amadeus. She knelt down and picked up a single pendant on a chain, holding it in her hand.

"Did I ever tell you why I hated the Obsidian of Ruby?" Lady asked, closing her hand around the gem.

"He destroyed your hometown," Amadeus said from somewhere behind her. She heard treasure shifting about, and clutched the pendant tighter to her chest. His voice was distant, but not cruel. It was more knowing than anything, and Lady squeezed the pendant in her hands. Amadeus continued, "And I believe you lost your father in the attack."

"I did," Lady said. She trembled, her eyes watering. Memories flooded her mind, unwanted. Black scales, and screams filled her mind. "My father was killed during the slaughter, and that monster mutilated his body with a shower of his wretched glass scales."

"So he did."

Lady continued, "He burned down the entire town, leaving nothing in his trail but broken homes. He took everything of value from my late mother's necklaces to the church's silver.

"While I consider myself lucky to have kept my eye," Lady breathed in through her teeth, "He took half of my face and left me with scars that will never go away."

"He did."

"But I vowed to kill him not because of that," Lady hissed. "Not because of trinkets and useless stones, but because he took everything of importance from me. He took my father!"

"He did," Amadeus repeated, a wet hoarseness in his voice that grabbed at Lady's heart.

"And worst of all," Lady said, spinning around and drawing her sword. She dropped the pendant from her hand while holding the chain. The word "Simon" written across the back glittered in the light, and Lady hissed. "He stole my heart."

Amadeus smiled weakly as his eyes changed from rich green to fiery red. "I did."

"How dare you," Lady hissed through a choked breath. The other man stood there, staring at her far too calmly. As the fire in her veins threatened to burn her from the inside out, he remained ice. She snarled, "It was you the entire time!"

"It was," Amadeus said, two large horns sprouting from his head like slowly growing vines. As he talked, familiar obsidian scales spread over his face, traveling down to his neck in a gentle wave. He reached up and undid the strap of his traveling cloak with an even gesture, flicking it off and resting it on the pile of treasure to his right. "But don't feel bad, I haven't met a slayer yet who's noticed."

"But that hasn't stopped dragons," Lady said, keeping her sword drawn and pointed at him. He dumped his armor on top of the traveling cape, without his usual care or effort. As if he couldn't be bothered. Lady twisted her grip on the sword, forcing her hand to stay still. "Martha knew what you were instantly. It's why she was so agitated, and why I caught you alone with her that night at the inn."

"Correct," Amadeus said, dropping his shirt on the ground after his armor. He rolled his naked shoulders as more scales grew along his skin, covering his chest and back. His smile dripped of fondness through the scales and growing fangs, and it was worse than anything Lady had ever experienced as it jabbed at her heart. "Care to make any other hindsight observations?"

"You got rid of the real Amadeus and took his place," Lady said, "that's why his mother won't speak to you."

"I did steal him away from her, that's true," Amadeus said, holding a hand over his heart and the other in the air to his side as he bowed at the chest. "You can fool the people, and you can fool the royalty, but you can never fool a mother."

Lady dropped the sword an inch, her mind turning in question after question. "Is her silence part of the deal with the rubies you have them giving you?"

"Yes," Amadeus said. He walked closer to her, and his eyes were laughing at her. He flexed his fingers, smooth fingers entered his palms, claws emerged. *How dare he be so amused?* Lady hissed to herself. Amadeus asked, "Anything else?"

Lady threw the emerald pendant at him, and he caught it with ease. He held it up and admired the gemstone, turning it over in his hand. "Did you kill Simon?"

"No, for once," he chuckled. He dropped the stone by the chain and tapped the pendant with his claw to spin the stone around in the air. "You and Nicholas had that honor."

Lady's eyes widened. "He was the Sandstone Dragon."

"He was," Amadeus tossed the emerald into the stack behind Lady. He laughed heartily, and licked his still sparkling white teeth with a forked tongue. "I'd been wanting that for quite some time, so I must thank you for getting it for me."

She held her sword with both hands, steadying it from her trembling. He smiled at her, with those same white teeth, and those deep eyes. The color had changed, but their expression had not. This man in a half-transformed state was Amadeus. The way he held himself, the way he looked at her. All of it was the same, no matter how his appearance changed. This monster was Amadeus.

The Obsidian of Ruby was Amadeus.

"I vowed to kill you," Lady said quietly. "I hate you."

"Do you?" Amadeus asked.

Lady cried out, thrusting the sword forward and through his heart. The glass scales that covered his chest shattered into pieces, covering the ground. She growled, and kept shoving it forward as he grabbed it, until she toppled the both of them over, her sword buried straight through him into the pile of gold behind his back.

"I don't. I don't. I don't." Lady sobbed, clutching to the handle of the sword. Amadeus was below her, his waist between her thighs. His hot blood covered her knees as it poured from the wound. It bubbled up around them, heating her armor until it burned, but Lady didn't care. Amadeus choked up a mouthful of blood, and his hands pawed at her legs. Lady whined, "I don't hate you at all."

"I didn't think that you did," Amadeus gasped, breathing heavily. He squeezed her thigh, his clawed fingers scratching against her armor.

"How could you?" Lady asked through the tears. She sniffed, rubbing her face on her her upper arm, smearing the wetness around her face. Amadeus lay there smiling at her, with those teeth and those wretched scales reminding her of what he was. What he had done. Lady screamed, "How could you make me love you?"

"I didn't," Amadeus whispered. He shifted, knocking loose a stack of coins behind him. "You fell in love all on your own."

"I vowed to kill you." Lady trembled. She ached everywhere, clutching to the sword she'd stabbed through his chest like a lifeline. "Promised my father I'd put your head on his grave and now look at me. Sobbing like a child."

"It's alright," Amadeus said. He reached up, and his blood covered hand scalded her unscarred cheek as he pressed his palm against her skin. It burned, his blood too hot. Everything was too hot. Lady leaned into it against her will, resting against his too warm hand. "I'll let you in on a secret, though."

Lady shivered as he sat up, dragging the sword farther through his ribs until only the hilt peeked out from his chest. Lady clung to the handle as he threw his arms around her. He hugged her tightly to his chest, squeezing hard enough Lady feared her ribs might break. The hilt dug into her waist, and she let go of it. Lady returned the embrace on instinct and breathed heavily as everything he touched burned. Amadeus whispered in her ear, "You missed my heart."

Wings ripped free from Amadeus' back, making the last sound Lady heard before everything went dark shattering glass.

To Be Continued

A Moment With Nicholas and Martha

"I WONDER HOW those other two are doing," Nicholas said, stretching his arms out high over his head. Martha watched him, wary of the way his eyes softened as he thought of those other two. Nicholas sat down on the inn bed, and leaned on the window sill. "I felt like a bit of a third wheel between the two of them every so often, but they were good friends. I rather miss them."

"I don't know how they are, and I don't care," Martha said, lounging on her back on the second bed on the far side of the rented room. She leaned on her side, flipping through a book and eating from a large stack of grapes, doing her best to pretend that Nicholas had not captured her focus. "They can both rot."

"Now that's not kind!" Nicholas insisted, still looking out the window. Martha had taken to using her human form more often now that he knew about it, but she refused to wear clothes. It let her keep a better eye on that idiot, and he needed it when he kept saying things like, "They were our friends."

"Amadeus was dangerous and Lady was an idiot," Martha said, crunching another grape. "That's all you need to know. We were in their company far too long as it was as far as I'm concerned."

"Dangerous?" Nicholas asked. A brown curl fell in his face as he turned his head in consideration. "I mean, I know he was a bit moody, but I wouldn't call him dangerous."

Martha popped one more grape into her mouth, and hopped off the bed. She strode across the room and wrapped her arms around his back. Nicholas flinched feeling her breasts through his thin shirt and counted to ten under his breath. It was far too easy to tease such a shy man. Martha hummed, setting her chin on his shoulder. "Trust me on this one. He was a bad, bad, boy."

"I think that you are just saying that to work me up," Nicholas said.

"I might be."

Martha leaned on his back, tightening her grip around his waist. She rubbed up and down against his stomach, thrilled at each nervous twitch he gave from the movement. Nicholas had no idea how close they had come to death while being with that man. She shivered, thinking of the first time she locked eyes with that monster.

The Obsidian of Ruby, standing in the middle of Honey Farms with a dragon slayer.

Martha had never feared for her life so badly than she had in that split second, and Nicholas the idiot couldn't tell. He couldn't see. He was wretchedly human and his eyes were closed to a dragon's disguises. She was a second from grabbing him and flying off when the Obsidian of Ruby gave that wretched warning for her to stay quiet. She obeyed, only because she didn't know what was going on. If he was there for something else, there was no need to draw extra attention to herself.

After a moment, it was clear he was there for the girl. It figured that Great Dragon was a pervert, lusting after some human woman. That was fine. She hardly cared what he did. But then Nicholas got himself involved and the Obsidian was angry.

He had been *jealous* of her Nicholas.

Martha still counted all of her lucky stars that they were alive and well after he threatened her late into the night while they were alone. She promised that she would keep Nicholas in check. Should he wander or step too close to the Obsidian's little human pet, she'd grab Nicholas and fly away. No harm, no foul, no hurt feelings for his woman.

That had been the deal.

She played it cool, of course, as they traveled together. The Obsidian of Ruby was playing human and enjoying himself, so there was no need to burst his bubble. Martha could handle it. But then, but then he showed up in the flesh. Fully transformed, the Great Dragon that terrified her.

After that fight, after seeing the real power that monster had, Martha vowed that she was going to get away. They weren't going to stay in that monster's company any longer with Nicholas constantly pressing his luck with those stupid hugs and knee knocks. The man couldn't keep his hands to himself, and ever time he hugged "Amadeus" Martha had an internal panic attack. Nicholas had been playing with fire and hadn't a clue. He'd hugged the Obsidian of Ruby plenty of times and lived, sure. But Martha knew better. Who knew how long it would take before that blasted dragon tired of his games and ate the lot of them for fun?

So she took her Nicholas and she left.

He could miss those two all he wanted.

Martha was never letting him go back.

"Martha dear," Nicholas said, swallowing and pushing lightly at her arm. "Would it really, really be too much trouble for you to find an outfit to wear when you did this?"

"What's the matter?" Martha said, flicking his ear with her finger. "I thought men liked to see naked women?"

"Some do, and some do not," Nicholas said, shifting away from her. Martha continued to hug him, amused he was more comfortable around a dragon that threatened to bite his head off than a soft woman in his bed. Nicholas swallowed, "And while you are very beautiful, ah, I would much appreciate it if you clothed yourself."

"Do I make you blush?"

"Yes," Nicholas swallowed. "Yes you do. You make me blush, and then I remember that you are my dragon, and then I sort of die a little inside. So please!"

Martha laughed and fell back onto the bed, letting him go. Her bare breasts bounced in the air, and she poked them upon catching him staring. "You're so ridiculous, Nicholas."

"Rhyming doesn't make it go away," he said, putting a pillow over her chest.

"I'm naked all the time," Martha said, shifting so that her naked hips bumped into his side. Nicholas shifted the pillow longways and looked out the window. Martha patted his hand. "I still don't see why now is so different."

"It just is!"

"Get some sleep, Nicholas," Martha said, crawling under the covers of his bed. She curled up in the soft blankets and sighed. "You're going to need it."

"Goodnight, Martha," He said, patting her on the side. He slipped off the bed and collapsed in the one across the room.

Martha watched him breathe and smiled, "Goodnight, Nicholas."

A Moment With Agatha

"LADY HAD BETTER appreciate all I do for her," Agatha said, applying her make up at her bedroom vanity. She added each line of color on her eyelids with care, making sure not a single hint of it was out of place. Agatha swapped out the thin paintbrush for her powders and thick brushes neatly organized on the counter space. "Finding a matching suit and dress in their sizes on the fly like that was not cheap!"

Agatha did wish them luck though, with every inch of her heart.

Lady was a good woman, who had always wanted a good man deep down. Agatha paused, applying her powder as she thought of the rather self-sufficient dragon slayer. Agatha shrugged, knowing that she was right, and continued with her make up routine. It was deep, *deep*, down, but it was there.

Agatha placed the compact on the table and stared at herself in the vanity mirror. Lady was the sort of woman who missed her father more than life itself, and desperately wanted another of him to love. Not in the sense that she wanted to marry her father, of course, but that she wanted a father in her life to love and adore children of her own. Let them have what she couldn't.

It was really quite sweet and touching, even if it had taken years of friendship for Agatha to figure it out.

Though Agatha did think that the man she found might be a little too close to her own father for comfort. Agatha bit the side of her lip, and pulled over a small packet from the side of her window. She pulled out a picture of Lady when she was a tiny little girl, standing next to her father.

Agatha had made a copy when her friend wasn't looking, knowing that Lady would never hand the precious surviving keepsake over on her own. Agatha felt bad about it for all of two seconds, but not enough to get rid of the picture.

The resemblance between Amadeus and Lady's father was uncanny.

Lady's father had also been a tall man with a thing for roses, if his shirt choices were any indication. He had dark hair and green eyes from what Agatha could see in the picture, and from what Lady had described the few brief times she mentioned him. From the photo, Agatha could tell that he was also quite handsome. Lady's mother had been a lucky woman.

Amadeus was tall, had dark hair, green eyes, and was most definitely handsome.

He was a perfect cut-out.

Agatha would have spoken up about it, had Amadeus not also been rich and the total opposite in personality from what Lady had described.

Her father had been warm, loving and friendly.

Amadeus was cold, calculating, and funny in that witty sort of way where he took great joy in mocking people.

He was only like Lady's father in looks alone, and Agatha had a feeling Lady never quite put it together in her own mind that Amadeus looked like her father. Lady only knew that she was attracted to him. Agatha almost didn't have the heart to tell her.

Besides, Amadeus was also rich.

Very, very filthy rich.

Agatha loved doing business with him. He was such a generous businessman, never complaining about full price or begging her for discounts. Now that was a real man.

And Lady deserved the very best.

So she had better appreciate everything that Agatha had done for her, and make sure to remember to drop Agatha's name often after she and Amadeus got married. Which they would of course.

Agatha had an eye for these things.

Those two were going to get hitched and have a small hoard of children under foot, or she'd sell off her jewelry business and eat her bonnet.

A Moment With Mother

THAT MONSTER HAD stolen her son.

She knew it was him, the dragon from the volcano. Who else could it have been? Others may have mocked her for jumping straight to that conclusion if she dared speak it out loud, but the old woman knew: The man that wore her dear Amadeus' face was none other than the Obsidian of Ruby that terrorized the continent and put fear into the lives of every child that she knew. He never had to say a word, but she knew the truth behind those green eyes.

She could see it in every smile, in every laugh, and in every time he kissed her on the head and called her "mother" with that slick voice of his. No matter how many times she almost wished she could forget and pretend that she had her little boy back, he would do something to remind her. And he would do it while smiling.

That dragon was more of a monster than anyone could ever give him credit for.

And he was not her son.

She was proud that she recognized the imposter immediately. He walked into the room the day after her real son had left the castle in a huff and disappeared for the evening. This stranger was a poor copy of her Amadeus. His armor was too clean, and his expression too smug.

Her boy had been a sniveling coward, and this man feared nothing.

The Obsidian of Ruby locked eyes with her, and in that moment, neither could hide anything from each other.

"You know," he had said, without a hint of surprise. Walking up to her chair. He knelt on one knee and touched her hand. His skin looked ice cold, but his touch was boiling hot on hers. "Don't you?"

"Is he dead?" She had asked, already knowing the answer.

"He's certainly never coming back," the dragon said. He reached up and straightened the brooch on her chest. She resisted the urge to smack him away, only because she could feel the power radiating from him. And she wanted answers. "I'm sorry to have stolen him away from you, but he was the closest I could match and replacing someone already high up in the ranks is much easier than starting anew as a nameless stranger, don't you agree?"

"Why are you here?" She asked.

"While I appreciate the sentiment of offering me treats and goodies once a month to bide my anger," the Obsidian said, "Your gifts and offerings could be better. If I pick out my own, then everyone wins, don't they?"

"You're a monster among monsters," she hissed. She pushed his hand away, no longer caring for her own life or his anger. "You took my son for that?"

"I did," he leaned up and kissed her on the forehead. He whispered into her skin, "And if you tell a single person, I'll take the lives of every single son and daughter in all of the Ruby Mines. Would you like them all to burn, or perhaps maybe I'll eat them instead?"

She had settled back into her chair, and grit her teeth. She wouldn't wish the agony of losing a child on anyone. "I won't tell a soul."

"I'm glad we can have this agreement."

"But you will never be my son, and I will never call you as such," She said, looking over her shoulder. The boy fixed his hair in the vanity mirror, rubbing down his eyebrows and exploring his face with his slim fingertips. Her son's face. She hissed. "I'd rather die."

"That's fine," the Obsidian of Ruby said, smiling with Amadeus' face. "Though you must forgive me if I call you 'Mother' from now on."

"I will not," she said, settling back into her chair. "I will never forgive you for what you've taken from me."

And she never did.

She had never forgotten.

Every loving gesture from him was poison. Every gift a curse, and every kiss to her head was torture. But she bore it all. This mother accepted all of his fake love and attention to keep their secret.

To protect the other little children of the town, and to keep their mothers from grieving the same, she bore this burden.

And held onto her grudge.

A Moment With Simon

THE OBSIDIAN OF Ruby was hugging him.

Every inch of his body cried out in terror as he was drawn into an embrace and called friend by one of the most terrifying and horrible of his kin. Simon wanted to sprint away and never look back, but something in the other dragon's tone of voice and hug was enough of a threat that he stilled and played along.

Two dragon slayers approached, which made him even more wary, and tales of gem dealers and friendships were sewn in an instant from the Obsidian of Ruby's lips.

Simon had no idea what was going on, but he knew that it was trouble. Trouble for him and trouble for everyone else, too. Probably.

There was nothing worse than a Great Dragon's boredom.

This particular boredom involved dragging Simon to a human's home, and forcing him to continue the act through dinner. The sheer oddness of it all was perhaps the only thing that kept Simon from planning an escape. Finding another dragon with them as well made it even weirder. The ruby scaled dragon gave him a look of pity, and Simon genuinely wondered what the Great Dragon was up to.

When they finally had a moment alone, he found his answers. The Obsidian of Ruby, or rather "Amadeus" as he was insisting, made up the story to keep Simon from blowing his cover with the two slayers.

That seemed fair enough, all considered.

Simon had certainly wanted to run screaming from the streets the second he saw the Great Dragon, which would have definitely hurt that whole cover thing he was trying for.

Most dragons when they took human form, only kept it for as long as they needed. Get in, find out where the humans kept their shiny things, get out and transform. Follow up by stealing the shiny things and then getting the heck out of there before a slayer showed up.

It often worked out pretty well.

The eldest dragons had made it an art form, even. Simon himself had done it enough that he'd learned to take a human name, and use little trinkets like his favorite necklace and good clothes to fit in better during the odd times he wanted to stay hidden.

The Obsidian of Ruby, however, well, that guy had always been a little odd.

He didn't just sneak around human towns, he had made a name for himself in one! The guy had gone total immersion and had an entire human life and family in addition to his looting and plundering on the side. A traveling merchant was quite the effective cover, if Simon could admit it to himself.

Now if only the Obsidian of Ruby would stop staring at his favorite emerald necklace. Or smirking at him.

He was planning something.

Simon shivered. That blasted Great Dragon was up to something, and all Simon knew was that he wanted no part in it.

The first opportunity he got, he was going to transform and go home and get away from this entire town. He'd move. That's what he'd do. He'd move far, far away.

And nothing was going to stop him.

A Moment With Amadeus

HIS MOTHER HAD always told him that he would never amount to anything. Amadeus clutched the the reins of his horse as they traveled across the valley. He was a coward, and always hid behind others with his problems. A weakling. A fool. A failure to his studies and his brand. Unfit to wear the name of First Family.

And oh, how she remind him of his short comings at every chance.

"Amadeus, you wear that shining silver armor but your inside are more suited to brass," she would often say. "You're nothing but a child playing pretend."

It always stung, like a knife to his heart.

Amadeus stopped his horse at the edge of the volcano edge, looking up at the towering mountain. This would be his moment. Amadeus would prove them all wrong. He climbed down from his horse, and his feet hit the ashy floor, just missing the flowers growing the fertile soil. He breathed in and breathed out slowly as his entire body quaked in fear.

He truly was a sniveling coward.

But if there was anyone who had the power to help him, it would be the dragon in this cave.

The legends, modern stories, and dragon slayers all said the same: dragons were only monsters and beasts. Intelligent demons that devoured all they could get their claws on, and greedy things that were slaves to their own lusts for treasure. Amadeus believed that those things were true, but there had to be more to them. If they were all so horrible, why were there some taken for pets or as steeds?

Amadeus felt it in his gut they were more than monsters. They possessed an odd and old magic that allowed them to take human shape if they so chose. If they could do that, who was to say that they couldn't do other great things?

Through the rocks and sharp turns, Amadeus climbed up the pathway to the great entrance. The smoke came clear from the opening in the side, a billowing tower signaling the Obsidian of Ruby was at home. Amadeus would walk past that threshold and talk to that dragon. He would. Amadeus sucked in a deep breath, hoping that it wasn't his last.

No one would ever call Amadeus of the Ruby Mines' First Family a coward again!

Amadeus walked through the dark entrance and far into the mountain until he entered the hoard room, every limb on his body trembling with more fear than he had ever experienced in his life. His footsteps echoed in the lit chamber, and he was careful not to touch a single coin or gem along his path, lest he awaken the dragon's wrath too early.

He wasn't that stupid.

"Hello? Obsidian of Ruby?" Amadeus swallowed, each trembling step an echo in the dark lair. Any possible etiquette he could have remembered left him as he spoke so casually to this giant monster. Amadeus swallowed deeply. It wasn't as if he had ever been good with his words anyway. "I'm sure you can hear me, so I'll try to make this short."

He heard a slide of treasure off to the left, and his teeth chattered in his head. "I am Amadeus of the Ruby Mines, First Family. I'm in charge of the gifts we bring you every month, and I was hoping to have a brief word with you."

"Speak," said a harsh and croaked voice from the back of the cave. He squinted, and saw the full form of the great dragon lounging on a bed of silver, nearly concealed by the darkness. The dragon was larger than anything Amadeus had ever seen in his life, and he stared at Amadeus with an amusement in his great red eyes that made the very small human want to turn tail and run as fast as he could. The dragon hissed, "Or leave."

"I'll speak! I'll speak!" Amadeus said, holding his hands up and stumbling forward a few more steps. He knocked into a stack of coins, spilling them over. Amadeus winced, and sucked in a breath as each coin fall echoed like a hammer in the room. The dragon kept watching him, and Amadeus relaxed his shoulders an inch as the last coin spun to a stop at his foot. He whispered, "I was wondering if you would do me a favor."

The dragon tilted his head, lifting it up from its resting place and Amadeus quickly added, "I'd pay you of course!"

The Obsidian of Ruby twirled a claw around, willing to at least humor Amadeus' request.

Amadeus took it as his opening. "I want to be brave. To be strong.

"I want everyone to know my name and stop being such an embarrassment to my household, but I do not know any way to do it," Amadeus bowed his head, wringing his hands together. He stared at the sparkling coins at his feet, feeling the tears well in the corner of this eyes. Everything in the room seemed to fall away as he spoke. "For they are right about everything they say. I am foolish, and I am a coward. I have no one else to turn to. If someone as great and powerful as you can not help me, I'm afraid I will have no choice but to suffer this way, forever shaming my mother."

"It will cost you," said a voice much closer, whispering in his ear. Amadeus looked up, and met his own green eyes staring back at him. The dragon had transformed into a human, and he had taken Amadeus' face as his own. It was like looking into a mirror, only the man that stared back at him looked brave and confident. Everything Amadeus had ever wanted to be. He hung on the dragon's ever word as he spoke, using Amadeus' voice in a way that he never imagined it could sound. "I can make your name great, and you will be respected above all others."

"Could you?" Amadeus asked, breathing in as he stayed locked with this man's gaze.

"For someone brave enough to come to me and ask for a favor, I think I can honor his request for something as insignificant as making his name known forever," he said. He tilted up Amadeus' chin and asked, "But are you willing to pay for it?"

Yes, please." Amadeus grabbed the dragon's hand in both of his own reverently, and kissed the knuckles. "Name your price and I will pay it."

"Very well," the dragon said.

He placed a kiss on Amadeus' forehead, and he felt peace, even as a clawed hand dug deep within his chest.

Everyone would know his name, and that was all that mattered when the world went dark.

Acknowledgements

To God be the glory forever, and ever, Amen.

As always: Thanks to God in the highest for the talent to write, and the push He gave to everyone who inspired me, helped me, and encouraged me. And of course, thanks be to God for giving us Jesus, who loves you & me.

At this particular moment: I want to thank my friends and family for sticking with me as I write. Their continued support, be it financially or encouragement in other ways, has been a lifesaver and I am truly grateful for all of them. I pray I can live up to expectations and continue writing as much as I can, as best as I can for as long as possible.

About The Author

Grey Liliy is a young woman who claims the East Coast of Virginia as her home. She enjoys anime, video games, movies, novels, and comics of just about any genre. Liliy has been drawing & writing a comic of her own since 2005, called *The Adventures of Wiglaf and Mordred*. Her debut novel, *Children of Hephaestus* was published in September 2012 and is available now.

www.ingramcontent.com/pod-product-compliance
Lightning Source LLC
Chambersburg PA
CBHW071520170626
46811CB00007B/2914